# big mouth
# & ugly girl

# big mouth & ugly girl

## JOYCE CAROL OATES

An imprint of HarperCollinsPublishers

The quotation on p. 120 is taken from
*The Obstacle Race: The Fortunes of Women Painters and
Their Work* by Germaine Greer (p. 319).

First published in the USA by HarperTempest 2002
First published in Great Britain by CollinsFlamingo 2003

3 5 7 9 8 6 4

CollinsFlamingo is an imprint of HarperCollins*Publishers* Ltd,
77-85 Fulham Palace Road, Hammersmith, London W6 8JB

The HarperCollins*Children's Books* website address is
www.harpercollinschildrensbooks.co.uk

ISBN 0 00 714573 X

Printed and bound in Great Britain by Clays Ltd, St Ives plc

TO Tara WEikum

# January

# ONE

**It was an** ordinary January afternoon, a Thursday, when they came for Matt Donaghy.

They came for him during fifth period, which was Matt's study period, in room 220 of Rocky River High School, Westchester County.

Matt and three friends – Russ, Stacey, Skeet – had formed a circle with their desks at the rear of the room and were conferring, in lowered voices, about Matt's adaptation of a short story by Edgar Allan Poe into a one-act play; after school, in Drama Club, the four of them were scheduled to read *William Wilson: A Case of Mistaken Identity* for the club members and their advisor, Mr Weinberg. It was a coincidence that Mr Weinberg, who taught English and drama at Rocky River High, was in charge of fifth-period study hall, and when a knock came at the door of the room, Mr Weinberg went to open it in his good-natured, sauntering manner.

"Yes, gentlemen? What can I do for you?"

Only a few students, sitting near the front of the room, took much notice. They might have registered a note of surprise in Mr Weinberg's tone. But Mr Weinberg, with his greying sandy hair worn longer than most of his male colleagues' at Rocky River, and a bristling beard that invited teasing, had a flair for dramatising ordinary remarks, giving a light touch where he could. Calling strangers "gentlemen" was exactly in keeping with Mr Weinberg's humour.

At the rear of the room, Matt and his friends were absorbed in the play, for which Matt was doing hurried revisions, typing away furiously on his laptop. Anxiously he'd asked his friends, "But does this *work*? Is it scary, is it funny, does it *move*?" Matt Donaghy had something of a reputation at Rocky River for being both brainy and a comic character, but secretly he was a perfectionist, too. He'd been working on his one-act play *William Wilson: A Case of Mistaken Identity* longer than his friends knew, and he had hopes it would be selected to be performed at the school's Spring Arts Festival.

Typing in revisions, Matt hadn't been paying any attention to Mr Weinberg at the front of the room talking with two men. Until he heard his name spoken – "Matthew Donaghy?"

Matt looked up. What was this? He saw Mr Weinberg pointing in his direction, looking worried. Matt swallowed hard, beginning to be frightened. What did these men, strangers, want with *him*? They wore dark suits, white shirts, plain neckties; and they were definitely not smiling. As Matt stared, they approached him, moving not together but along two separate aisles, as if to block off his route if he tried to escape.

Afterwards Matt would realise how swift and purposeful – and practised – they were. *If I'd made a break to get my backpack... If I'd reached into my pocket...*

The taller of the two men, who wore dark-rimmed glasses with green-tinted lenses, said, "You're Matthew Donaghy?"

Matt was so surprised, he heard himself stammer, "Y-Yes. I'm – Matt."

The classroom had gone deathly silent. Everyone was staring at Matt and the two strangers. It was like a moment on TV, but there were no cameras. The men in their dark suits exuded an authority that made rumpled, familiar Mr Weinberg in his corduroy jacket and slacks look ineffectual.

"Is something w-wrong? What do you want with – me?"

Matt's mind flooded: something had happened at home to his mother, or his brother, Alex... his father was away on business; had something happened to him? A plane crash...

The men were standing on either side of his desk, looming over him. Unnaturally close for strangers. The man with the glasses and a small fixed smile introduced himself and his companion to Matt as detectives with the Rocky River Police Department and asked Matt to step outside into the corridor. "We'll only need a few minutes."

In his confusion Matt looked to Mr Weinberg for permission – as if the high school teacher's authority could exceed the authority of the police.

Mr Weinberg nodded brusquely, excusing Matt. He too appeared confused, unnerved.

Matt untangled his legs from beneath his desk. He was a tall, lanky, whippet-lean boy who blushed easily. With so many eyes on him, he felt that his skin was burning, breaking into a fierce flamelike acne. He heard himself stammer, "Should I – take my things?" He meant his black canvas backpack, which he'd dropped on to the floor beside his desk, the numerous messy pages of his play script, and his laptop computer.

Meaning too – Will I be coming back?

The detectives didn't trouble to answer Matt, and didn't wait for him to pick up the backpack; one of them took charge of it, and the other carried Matt's laptop. Matt didn't follow them from the room; they walked close beside him, not touching him but definitely giving the impression of escorting him out of study hall. Matt moved like a person in a dream. He caught a glimpse of his friends' shocked faces, especially Stacey's. Stacey Flynn. She was a popular girl, very pretty, but a serious student; the nearest Matt Donaghy had to a girlfriend, though mostly they were "just friends", linked by an interest in Drama Club. Matt felt a stab of shame that Stacey should be witnessing this.... Afterwards he would recall how matter-of-fact and practised the detectives obviously were, removing the object of their investigation from a public place.

What a long distance it seemed, walking from the rear of the classroom to the front, and to the door, as everyone stared. There was a roaring in Matt's ears. Maybe his house had caught on fire? No, a plane crash... Where was Dad, in Atlanta? Dallas? When was he coming home? Today, tomorrow? But was it likely that police would come to school to inform a student of such private news?

It was bad news, obviously.

"Through here, son. Right this way."

In the corridor outside the classroom, Matt stared at the detectives, who were both big men, taller than Matt and many pounds heavier. He swallowed hard; he was beginning now to feel the effect of a purely physical anxiety.

Matt heard his hoarse, frightened voice. "What – is it?"

The detective with the glasses regarded Matt now with a look of forced patience. "Son, you know why we're here."

# two

That January afternoon, when Ugly Girl struck out.

Not that I was hurt, *I was not.*

Not that I gave a damn, *I did not.*

Not that any of you saw me cry, *nobody ever saw Ugly Girl cry.*

All through school, if I'd had to wait to be chosen for any team, I'd have waited at the sidelines like the other left-behind losers. Fat girls, girls wearing thick glasses, girls lacking "motor coordination", asthmatic girls who puffed and panted if they had to trot a few yards. But Ugly Girl was one of the best athletes at Rocky River High. Even the guys had to acknowledge that fact, however they hated to. So Ms Schultz, our gym teacher (kind of an Ugly Girl herself, big boned, clumsy in social situations, with coarse swarthy skin and kinky hair), always named me a team captain. She'd call out "Ursula Riggs" like she hadn't any idea the name was ugly, and even when she chided me – "Ursula, be careful!" – "Ursula, that's a foul!" – you could tell she favoured me, in secret. *Ugly Girls got to stick together, right?*

In seventh and eighth grades I was a swimmer-diver, and that was my happiest time. But swim team didn't work out. Ugly Girl's body wasn't built for the diving board, or for water. Or for critical eyes. In high school I got into "land" sports – "contact" sports. Soccer, field hockey, volleyball, basketball. There Ugly Girl excelled. Junior year I was captain of the Rocky River girls' basketball team. We were on a winning streak, though I surely wasn't what you'd call a popular captain, and if I was in one of my Fiery Red moods, I wasn't what you'd call a team player. I was out to score, and I scored.

Ms Schultz scolded me, in the way that teachers who like you can scold, letting you know they expect more of you than you're giving. "You're a gifted athlete, Ursula, and I know that you're a very good academic student too. When you want to be." Pause. "I wish I could rely upon you more, with your teammates." I didn't like hearing this, but I just shrugged and stared at the floor. My clunky feet. Ugly Girl wished she could rely upon herself more too.

I didn't have many friends in Rocky River. (My mom and little sister were into "friends".) But that was a Boring Fact.

Strange: how stuff that used to bother me in middle school, had the power to make me hide away and cry, didn't bother me at all now. Since that day I woke up and knew I wasn't an ugly girl, I was Ugly Girl.

I laughed, and it wasn't a nice feminine laugh like my mom encourages. It was a real laugh, deep in the gut.

9

I would never be ashamed of my body again; I would be proud of it. (Except maybe my breasts. Which I strapped in like I was on swim team, and kind of flattened, in a sports bra.)

My hair used to be this pretty fluffy blonde, the baby pictures show. Now it's darker. For the hell of it someday I'd like to shave my skull, like a skinhead. Or maybe trim my hair in a crew cut. Or dye it black. Or bleach it. Except my dad wouldn't approve and my mom would die of shame. They had their prissy notions of *girl* like my kid sister, Lisa. Lisa is an aspiring ballerina, and Mom's gaga about her dancing classes.

What pissed me was until just recently my Grandma Riggs was into comparing Lisa and me. "Ursula, dear, when are you going to *stop growing*?" Like this was a joke, or something I could control by an act of will, which made me hate the Grandma Riggs I used to love.

Why do old people who've known you since infancy think they actually *know you* and can say insulting things?

"I'll stop growing, Grandma," I said, trying to keep it pleasant, "when you stop getting older. OK?"

That was mean. That hurt Grandma. Ugly Girl didn't care.

Lots of people I was starting to hate who I used to like a lot. But when you like people, you can be hurt. I'd made a few mistakes with girl friends, and one or two guys I'd thought were my buddies, and I wouldn't make these mistakes again.

What I liked about being so tall was I could look just about any guy eye-to-eye, even older guys on the street, or actual adult men I didn't know. Unlike other girls, I didn't shrink away like a balloon deflating if guys teased me or said crude things meant to embarrass. How do you embarrass Ugly Girl, exactly?

Around school you hear girls talking about their boyfriends, certain "sexual practices" expected of them, sometimes right in the school building, or in the parking lot behind; and hearing such things made Ugly Girl just laugh. As if Ugly Girl would *go down* for any guy, or any human being, ever!

I'd grown taller than my mom by the time I was thirteen, and I really liked that. Mom was one of those "petite" women who watch their weight constantly, and are anxious about lines and sagging in their faces, as if the whole world is staring at them and *cares!* It felt good, too, to be almost as tall as my dad (who was six feet three, weighed over two hundred pounds), so he'd have to treat me more like an equal than just a child.

Most of all it felt good to be as tall as, in some cases taller than, my teachers. Not one of the Rocky River female teachers was Ugly Girl's height, and always I made sure I stood straight, like a West Point cadet, when I spoke with them. Everyone was cautious around Mrs Hale, our guidance counsellor, who could sabotage your chances of getting into a good college by putting something negative in your file, but not Ugly Girl. My favourite teachers were Ms Zwilich, who taught biology, and Mr Weinberg, who taught literature, and I wasn't afraid to stand up to them, either.

I could see that my teachers didn't know what to make of me. There was Ursula Riggs, who was an excellent student, a serious girl with an interest in biology and art, and there was Ugly Girl, who played sports like a Comanche and who had a sullen, sarcastic tongue. It was Ugly Girl who was susceptible to "moods" – these ranged from Inky Black to Fiery Red. In a mood I'd sometimes walk out of class, yawning; or I might quit a test in the middle, just snatch up my backpack and exit. My grades were everything from A+ to F. In a rational frame of mind I knew I had to worry I'd screw up my SATs and not get into a college of the calibre I could bear going to, but then in the next minute I'd shrug and laugh. *Who cares? Not Ugly Girl.*

Ursula Riggs was a coward, fearing other people's opinions and the future. Ugly Girl was no coward, and didn't give a damn about the future. *Ugly Girl, warrior-woman.*

Sure, I knew people talked about me behind my back. My mom and dad. My classmates, even my so-called friends. Pushing along the corridor at school, entering the cafeteria – I saw the eyes, I heard the whispers, muffled laughter. *Ursula! Ugly Ursula.* I knew, and I didn't care. As long as they stayed out of my way, right?

A Fiery Red mood was great for basketball – Ugly Girl really burned up the court – but an Inky Black wasn't so good. An Inky Black meant that my feet were concrete blocks, and where my eyes used to be, there were these broken little pieces of glass that hurt. I tried to avoid the Inky Blacks by slinking away and drawing in my notebook, charcoal sketches of invented people or scenes of my favourite place, the Rocky River Nature Preserve, or if I needed a desperate remedy I'd go running, for miles, in the nature preserve, running-running-running in any kind of weather until I practically collapsed. *Ugly Girl, run to earth.* But it felt good, mostly.

I hated changing clothes in the locker room, which was a lonely place for me, an awkward place; I'd get almost as self-conscious about my body as I'd been in eighth grade, and the other girls giggling and whispering together, like in a weird way they were all sisters, and closer to my sister Lisa than they'd ever be to me. But as soon as I shut my locker and ran out into the gym, on to the basketball court, where every smell was so right, and the glare of the overhead lights on the polished floor, I could feel the Fiery Red coming up. Here was my place! I loved basketball, and if my teammates played well, if they passed the ball to Ugly Girl to score, and didn't trip over their own feet too much, I loved them too – or anyway liked them.

"Hey. You weren't bad, you guys. Thanks."

These words Ugly Girl had been known to mutter, after just a few games. The Rocky River team was thrilled to hear them, even those girls who hated their captain's guts.

Then it happened. This jinxed game with our archrivals Tarrytown.

It was a Thursday afternoon in January, our first game of the new year, at home, and right away I saw that my team wasn't behind me. Even my stronger players were clumsy and slow, leaving me unprotected at crucial moments. Every time I sank a basket and brought Rocky River ahead, one of the girls messed up, lost the ball, and Tarrytown leaped ahead. My own team was sabotaging me! Tarrytown was one of the most competitive girls' basketball teams in the district – they'd beaten us in the district play-offs last year, maybe they were out-psyching us? But not Ursula Riggs. I was hot to play. In my maroon jersey and shorts, my body thrumming with excitement, I had unlimited energy – ready to ignite! Fiery Red had been building up for hours, now the fire was flaring up, up into my skull, and the more baskets I scored, the more I wanted to score. Even people who disliked Ugly Girl had to concede I was hot, and applauded my moves.

What pissed me: the game hadn't drawn much of a crowd from the school. There were almost as many Tarrytown supporters as Rocky River supporters – and they were loud in their enthusiasm for their team. We had maybe one twentieth of the Friday-evening crowds that turned out for the guys' games, and the irony was we were better than the guys, on a winning streak while the guys had lost as many as they'd won. We deserved more respect than we were getting. My mother hadn't showed up, either, when she'd halfway promised she might "drop in". Mom had even planned on bringing Lisa – "If our schedules work out." Still, we did have supporters, spread out on the bleachers, and the team owed them a good game.

Maybe a few times I lost my temper and said some sharp things to the girls, and they resented it, and by the final quarter nobody was speaking to me, or even looking at me if they could help it. The score was 28–27, Tarrytown ahead; it was 30–31, Rocky River ahead; it was 33–30, Tarrytown ahead. (Of Rocky River's points, Ugly Girl must've scored all but four or five.) As the game neared its end, we were sweating, and panting, and exhausted, and I'd gotten a little rough with two or three of the Rocky River girls – "accidentally". It made me see red that the Tarrytown girls were rallying, playing together like a real team, scoring points that roused cheers and whistles from their supporters while ours sat sullen and dissatisfied. Tarrytown went into the lead by six points after a stupid blunder by our "star" guard, and during a break I told Ms Schultz I was quitting, and she snapped at me, oh no you don't, Ursula, don't you dare, if you quit I'll have you expelled. Schultz was the only one who wouldn't take shit from Ugly Girl, she was one tough woman I had to respect. So I splashed cold water on to my burning face and went back into the game, and for a few minutes we managed to keep Tarrytown from scoring. By sheer luck I snatched the ball from the Tarrytown star forward, a dark-skinned African-American girl my height and size, and I was charged with adrenaline running down the court when suddenly, it was like being struck by lightning, I was tripped by somebody's foot, and falling, falling hard, my right knee striking the floor, and the ball was snatched from me and passed to the Tarrytown forward, who runs, leaps like a gazelle, and scores, easy as a knife cutting into soft butter. From their side of the gym, cheers; from our side, groans. My face is burning, I know everyone is blaming me. Because Ugly Girl played so well until now, it looks as if she's coasting, or hanging back. I'm running, limping. I'm shouting for the ball. My right knee is throbbing with pain, both my knees are weak as water. What's happening to me? I never look towards the bleachers, but I'm seeing the derisive eyes, jeering faces, hands mock clapping. The Rocky River kids are yelling at me, I can almost hear them – "Ursula! Ug-ly Ur-sula!" Their faces are blurred as if they're underwater, or maybe it's sweat running into my eyes and stinging. A terrible sick feeling churns in my stomach. The way I felt years ago at a swim meet when I froze at the edge of the diving board, just stopped cold, and there was dead silence, and I bit my lower lip trying not to cry as finally I turned and walked away, to my shame and humiliation. *But this is Ugly Girl. This is not a scared eighth grader.*

I throw myself back into the game, the last minutes are ticking by, I'm leaping for the ball as it flies overhead. And I've got it! Even with my blurred eyes, my shaky legs, I've got it. Even as I'm tasting vomit at the back of my mouth. People are screaming at me, I'm about to score, but suddenly the ball is stolen from me, now I'm desperate to reclaim it, running, skidding, breathing through my mouth like a winded horse. I'm tripped again – but refuse to fall. I'm running, beneath the basket, a clear shot, I send the ball spinning a fraction of an inch from the rim so it strikes the backboard, damn it, at the wrong angle, and ricochets back, and a fantastically high-jumping Tarrytown guard grabs it and runs down the court, passes it to the forward, who scores. The game is almost over. The gym is deafening with cheers, boos, whistles, applause, and foot stamping. Ugly Girl is reeling, knees like water. What has happened to Ugly Girl? There's a collision of several girls, grunts and thuds, I'm sprawling on the floor writhing in pain, biting my lower lip to keep it in. Thank God for the referee's whistle – "Foul!"

Suddenly facing the basket, at the foul line. How many times I've practised foul shots here in the gym, coached by Ms Schultz, I can do them in my sleep. I can do them blind. Except, suddenly, I'm trembling. I'm scared I will be sick to my stomach. I'm scared the ball isn't my friend this afternoon, but my enemy. This game is jinxed and Ugly Girl is jinxed.

There are titters from the bleachers. In my hazy vision I can see Ms Schultz's tense face. The Tarrytown team in blue jerseys and the Rocky River team in maroon are staring hard at me, in that instant I can read their thoughts: *Ugly Girl, fail! We hate you.* And Ugly Girl is scared. Her uniform is soaked in sweat, she can smell her panicked body. She bounces the ball a few times to psych herself up. As if nothing is wrong. Carefully she grips the ball in both hands, curves it in towards her chest and up, and out – the ball flies to the backboard, strikes it hard, and bounces harmlessly off.

Titters, groans. Silence.

Ugly Girl swallows down vomit. Ugly Girl stands favouring her left leg. Ugly Girl bounces the ball again, one, two, three – and again throws. Shutting her eyes like a beginner.

The second shot falls short.

*Ugly Girl strikes out.*

I hear waves of boos, anger, and disgust from my teammates, I see Schultz's look of fury. There's no mistaking the message I'm being sent.

They think I lost the game for Rocky River on purpose.

# three

**life consists of** Facts, and Facts are of two kinds: Boring, and Crucial.

I figured this out for myself in eighth grade. Wish I could patent it!

A Boring Fact is virtually any fact that doesn't concern you. Or it's just trivial, a nothing fact. (Like the annual rainfall in, let's say, Bolivia. Crucial to the Bolivians, but Boring to everyone else.)

I know the Crucial Facts of Ugly Girl's life are Boring Facts to others. Yet, to Ugly Girl, they are Crucial.

There's one test of a Crucial Fact: it hurts.

"I didn't. I didn't screw up on purpose. But if you want to think I did, Ms Schultz, think it!"

The way I uttered *Mzzzzz*, it was a snarl.

I ran limping from the gym, into the locker room. I would hide in the farthest shower, like a dog licking its wounds.

*Ugly Girl, sabotaging her own team.*

*Ugly Girl, we'll never forgive you.*

Could I blame them? Maybe they were right.

I turned the hot water on hot as I could bear. Burn, burn! Ugly Girl, a traitor to Rocky River. The water was scalding, steaming. Maybe my skin would turn pink like a lobster's and peel off.

The remainder of the game, two or three minutes, had passed like a dream. Rocky River lost by three points. Ms Schultz gripped my shoulder like her fingers were pinchers. "Ursula. I'd like to speak with you."

I had fled the gym. The sullen hateful faces. Tarrytown's exulting, screaming supporters.

Yes: the outcome of any sporting event is a Very Boring Fact to all persons not involved with the sporting event.

But it is a Crucial Fact to those involved.

I would not quickly forget the shiny-faced girls glaring at me. Ms Schultz among them. My eyes were stinging with tears. But I would give none of my accusers the satisfaction of seeing me cry.

In the shower, the hot tears spilled out. Or maybe it was just the hot, hot water streaming down my face.

How was it my fault, that we lost the game? When I'd scored most of the points?

*Yes, but you know: it is your fault.*

*You wanted to punish them. And yourself.*

I would quit the team! They hated Ursula Riggs – let them see how they would do without me.

Maybe I would transfer to another school. A private school in Manhattan.

It was an easy commute. Dad commuted – maybe I could ride with him.

I let the shower run cold, icy cold. To punish. My teeth chattering and skin puckered in goose bumps.

I hid in the farthest shower. The other girls knew I was there, I could hear their voices and sullen, sardonic laughter at a distance. Not once did I hear the name "Ursula", but I'm sure I heard "she" – "her" – repeated numerous times, in tones of disgust.

I heard locker doors being slammed, hard. No one called out to me, to say goodbye.

Not even Bonnie LeMoyne, who I'd thought was sort of my friend.

Not even Ms Schultz, who must've known what I was feeling.

*It wasn't my fault! Please believe me.*

Like oil spillage, an Inky Black mood was oozing up into my skin. The exulting Fiery Red had quickly faded, on the basketball court. When I'd been tripped, and fallen. *Ugly Girl, down.*

I would live and relive the closing minutes of the Tarrytown game, I knew. Like my recurring nightmare of freezing – in public – at the swim meet in eighth grade.

At least this time Mom wasn't in the audience to be shocked, disappointed.

At least Mom hadn't brought Lisa to witness her big sister's humiliation.

It was a relief, actually, that Dad never came to watch me play any sports. He'd missed most of the swim meets, and there was never much pretence he could take time off from work to see my high school games. Even if Dad wasn't out of the country on business, he was consumed by work in New York. He was CEO of the Drummond Corporation on Park Avenue, Manhattan, which had branches in London, Paris, Rome, Frankfurt, Tokyo and Buenos Aires.

Of course, Dad had time to see Lisa dance in *The Nutcracker* last month.

But that's different. Ballerinas are beautiful to watch. Not sweaty, grunting, ugly.

Dad was always asking me, "How're things going, Ursula?" with a frowning smile and that special concern in his eyes that made me want to believe he was truly interested, but I'd long ago learned not to tell him anything genuine, let alone in detail, because his eyes would glaze over, he'd get restless, glancing around for Mom to rescue him. Almost anything I said, he'd say, "Swell, honey! Sounds good. Keep it up."

Did I blame my dad? No. I knew there was nothing in my life of genuine interest or importance. I was a Boring Fact. Sure, Dad would care, Dad would care *a lot*, when I began to apply for college, but that wasn't until next year. (Though he'd been talking about "my daughter Ursula" going to Harvard, where he'd gone. Harvard: the Number One Cliché.) In the meantime, Dad had his own life. It didn't involve even Mom much any more. He was Clayton Riggs, Clay to his friends, a busy, important man. Workaholic, and proud of it. There were kids at Rocky River High whose dads worked for my dad at Drummond, which was kind of embarrassing. Dad's truest life was elsewhere, not confined to our six-bedroom white colonial in Rocky River, even if that house was his and Mom's "dream house" on three acres of prime real estate.

Sure, I'd cared when I was younger. Before I was Ugly Girl.

By the time I left the shower, the locker room was dead silent. I towelled my hair dry over a sink. Combed out snarls with swift, fierce tugs of my steel comb. Avoiding my reflection in the mirror. My skin was reddened from the water but I was feeling a little better. I'd scoured away my rage and hurt. No one had seen Ugly Girl cry, and no one ever would.

*Ugly Girl stands alone.*

The locker room was a safe place, deserted. I liked the special smells, the steamy warmth. I didn't have to not-hear the other girls talking and laughing together, sharing secrets. I didn't have to notice them falling silent when I dialled my lock combination, and banged open my locker the way I usually did.

When I got home, Mom would smile guiltily at me and ask how was the game and in the same breath apologise for missing it and I would say the game was OK, Mom, you didn't miss much. So her guilty smile could fade. So she could fuss over pretty sparrow-boned Lisa.

Still, I had to go home. I couldn't hide in the damned locker room all night.

I dressed quickly, carelessly. Throwing on clothes. My jeans I'd been wearing for weeks, and a loose-fitting black-flannel (man's) shirt. Sometimes, out of perversity, I wore a loose-fitting white (man's) shirt, for a funky-formal look. A row of gold studs in my right earlobe. Though scorning style, Ugly Girl had style. In ninth grade I'd "tattooed" on my left biceps, in coloured inks, a mean-looking snake coiled about the motto DON'T TREAD ON ME, which caused a sensation at school until I was made to wash it off.

Everywhere I could, I wore my soiled old Mets cap.

It drove my mom crazy. Even my dad, who liked baseball, winced.

"At least the Yankees, honey? Why the *Mets*?"

If you have to ask, Dad, you won't ever know.

It was late, past five o'clock. A thundery-dark winter sky outside. By now Rocky River High would be mostly deserted, I thought. (I hoped.) Sports events and practices and club meetings would be over, the school buses would be gone. It was strange to be the last one leaving the locker room; usually I was the first. When we won a game, there was a giddy, celebratory feeling – which Ugly Girl shared in, to a degree. But only briefly. Then I'd walk out, alone. Not even waiting for Bonnie. I liked being the first to leave. I knew they would be praising my performance, regardless of what they thought of *me*. But tonight everything was weird. It was like the world had turned inside out. I had a sickish flash of myself standing tall and gawky and trembling at the foul line, the basketball (that should've been my friend but was my enemy) gripped in my sweaty hands. All those eyes on me. *Ug-ly Ursula!* They'd wanted me to fail, and I had.

"It wasn't my fault. It *was not*."

I wanted to shout this in Ms Schultz's face.

I refused to be one of those neurotic girls who make themselves sick feeling guilty for what isn't their fault.

Still, I didn't much want to leave the locker room. Where it

23

was safe. I could see why a wounded animal creeps away to hide. My knee was hurting again, and all my bones felt cracked. My guts swirled with that sick flu feeling. Maybe it was only flu? I hoped so, not the symptoms of an Inky Black mood coming on.

*Ugly Girl! We'll never forgive you.*

"Ursula? Did you *hear—*?"

It was Bonnie LeMoyne calling to me.

I was leaving school and surprised to see so many people standing by the rear entrance, talking together in lowered, excited voices. What was this? Bonnie, and other girls from the team. Even Ms Schultz. People who'd been at the game. And others. At first I thought there'd been an accident out in the parking lot.

Bonnie waved and called out to me like nothing was wrong.

"Did I hear what? What's going on?" I asked.

Bonnie said, "Nobody knows, for sure. A bomb—"

"A *bomb*?"

"Well, maybe."

There was a rumour that a bomb threat had been called in to the school that afternoon. Or maybe an actual bomb had been discovered in the cafeteria, or – the library? A boy said he'd heard that the bomb – "a pipe bomb" – had been found in a custodian's closet near the gym. "When? When was this?" I asked sceptically. "Wouldn't our game have been called, and the school evacuated?" But no one paid much attention to me. They were talking all at once, their faces glowing. Some senior girls joined us with the news. They'd just heard that a boy, a junior, had brought a handgun to school, or – a .22 rifle? – or maybe it was a machine gun that could spray hundreds of bullets in a few seconds? Someone said he'd heard that the boy had been arrested, taken out of his fifth-period class by armed cops. "In Rocky River *High*? Armed *cops*?" We were all astonished. Here the girls' basketball team had been playing Tarrytown, oblivious of such an emergency! A perverse kind of elation passed through us, like an electric current. I was talking with people I hardly knew. Ms Schultz was in the group, and talking with me, too, as if she hadn't been disgusted with me an hour before.

Some boys were saying that our principal, Mr Parrish, had disarmed the student and called police – or had Mr Parrish been held at gunpoint in his office, and had to be rescued? Someone said he'd heard it was Mr Weinberg. Everyone was talking at once. A girl was saying she'd seen Stacey Flynn at her locker, pale and crying, on her way home early – "But Stacey wouldn't say a word to me, what was wrong." Maybe she'd been threatened by the gunman? The more we speculated, the more excited we became. It was like a lighted match set to dried grass.

Some senior boys appeared, one of them Trevor Cassity, the football player, a popular, aggressive guy whose father happened to work for my dad. There was an awkward feeling between Trevor and me because of this fact, a kind of mutual embarrassment, and resentment, too, on Trevor's part, for Ugly Girl was a girl who would've been beneath Trevor's contempt as a sex object – except for these mitigating circumstances. So Trevor Cassity and Ursula Riggs instinctively avoided each other when they happened, not very frequently, to meet. Now Trevor and his buddies were animated, indignant. Had we heard it was Matt Donaghy, a junior, who'd been threatening to blow up the school and "massacre" as many people as he could, had we heard he'd been *arrested*?

Matt Donaghy! This had to be wrong.

I protested, "I don't believe you. Matt wouldn't do such a crazy thing."

"Well, he did. He *tried.*"

Now, I didn't know Matt Donaghy very well, but I'd been in school with him since fifth grade. This year he was in just one class with me, Mr Weinberg's. He was in with a popular clique of juniors, not at the centre of the clique, maybe, but towards the edge. It was my impression he had lots of friends, and girls liked him. A "wit" – a "clown" – a "wise guy" – but his humour wasn't mean or malicious. As far as I knew, Matt Donaghy wouldn't make jokes to embarrass girls, or say crude things like lots of other guys did. Matt Donaghy, threatening to blow up the school! Bringing a bomb to school, or a gun! It was just too crazy. Matt had never talked back to any teacher, he'd never said anything sarcastic, in my memory.

I said these things, and some people quickly agreed with me, but others disagreed. "Matt's a computer nut, that's the type. They contact each other on the Internet." "Matt isn't into computers. That's Skeet." "Skeet too. Probably they're all in it." "Russ Mercer, too? They aren't arrested – are they?" "Look, none of these guys are the type, this has got to be wrong. It must be somebody else—" "What's the type that does this stuff? Blow up schools?" "The shy quiet type. Y'know – repressed." "That's not Matt Donaghy. He's got a wild sense of humour. He's a class officer, for God's sake."

One of Trevor's buddies was saying that he'd been told by a "reliable source" that two senior girls had heard Matt Donaghy talking in the cafeteria at lunchtime, saying he was going to blow up the school, and they reported him. "Like, Donaghy had this plan to kill as many people as he could, including teachers, because he was pissed over some grade he got on a test – or something he wrote, that got turned down by the newspaper."

"That's ridiculous," I said. "That is *not true.*"

Trevor Cassity stared at me. "How do you know?"

"Because I was there."

They were all looking at me, challenging me. Suddenly I felt revulsion for these people, worse than I'd felt after the basketball game.

I turned and walked away. Fast.

A few people called after me, wanting me to come back, but there was Trevor Cassity saying in his low, mocking voice, "Sure! It's just like big Ursula to butt in where she doesn't know shit." I could have kept going, pretended I didn't hear, but I stopped and called back, with as much dignity as I could manage since I was trembling with anger, "You're the ones who're butting in where you don't know shit. *I* don't believe any of this."

I turned and began to run. Fresh, cold air! A feathery snowfall was swirling around me like a blessing. My face was burning, and my heart pumped adrenaline. It just disgusted me how people who knew Matt Donaghy, or should've known him and trusted him, were willing to believe such things.

Worse, they were almost gloating about it. Like a lynch mob.

# four

"SON, YOU KNOW why we're here."

"I... do?"

"Do you have anything to say to us, maybe? Anything you'd like to get off your chest?"

"I... don't know." He was frightened, his mind wasn't working right. None of this made sense to him, yet (it seemed) it made sense to the Rocky River detectives. They were adult men, severe-looking men, why would they have come to the high school to speak with him, except for a reason? He saw (in the corner of his eye, hadn't wanted to acknowledge) that Mr Parrish, the school principal, was standing a few yards away, in the corridor, just standing there, waiting. Why?

Matt began to stammer. His heart was fluttering like a small crazed bird trapped in his chest. "Is something wrong at... home? Did something happen to... my mom?"

The detectives exchanged a quick, inscrutable glance. As if this were a new idea to them. Both spoke:

"*Did* something happen to your mom, Matt?"

"Yes, son? *Did* something happen at home?"

It was then Matt Donaghy began to panic. Something was wrong with his breathing. His lungs seemed to shut down. A wide-winged black-feathered bird bigger than any eagle rose up behind him and brought its wings down over him, shutting out his vision, stopping his heart.

# five

NO I did not. I did not. I DID NOT.

*I did not say those things, and I did not plan those things.*
*Won't anyone believe me?*

Matt Donaghy had not been arrested by Rocky River police.

Matt Donaghy had not been handcuffed and led forcibly from the rear of Rocky River High to a waiting police vehicle and taken to police headquarters to be charged with any crime.

No one had been a witness to such a spectacle. But it would be talked of as if it had happened. It would be talked of, and shared, and discussed like a scene in a movie that not everyone had seen, but a few had seen, or claimed to have seen, and by being talked of with such zest, such dread and enthusiasm, it would shortly come to seem that, at Rocky River High, nearly everyone had seen it, and had opinions about it.

"He was cuffed? Matt was *cuffed*?"

"Not his ankles, though. So he could walk."

Had Rocky River police actually entered the school? During fifth period? Those classmates of Matt's who'd seen the plainclothes detectives lead him out of study hall would describe the men in varied ways, disagreeing on details, but all agreed that the detectives had been wearing suits, and had spoken quietly to Matt.

What happened outside the classroom was a matter for speculation.

It began to be claimed that the plainclothes detectives had been backed up by uniformed, armed cops. It began to be claimed that there'd been a SWAT team with high-powered rifles, bulletproof masks, and vests. Few could truthfully claim to have seen the SWAT team on the premises, though the building wasn't exactly deserted at the time Matt was led out of study hall.

Where had the detectives taken Matt exactly? Some believed that they'd all gone downstairs to Mr Parrish's office, and had left for police headquarters later; others, impatient with such an inessential detail, insisted that Matt had been "arrested" immediately and taken away to headquarters.

"If he'd made a break for it, they would've shot him? Wow."

"No way Matt was gonna make a break. They had him, and he knew it."

"Did they search his locker? Did they confiscate stuff?"

"Did he confess?"

"Did you ever see any gun of Matt's, like in his locker?"

"I didn't know Matt had guns."

"Stuff to make bombs? Or, like plans? Drawings?"

"They'd be downloaded from the Internet. All that kind of shit you can download if you know where to look."

In Mr Parrish's office, the door shut tight.

Matt's teeth were chattering. He tried to speak calmly.

"Look, this is crazy. I never... what you're saying."

"We've had a report, Matt. Two reports. Two witnesses. They heard you."

"Heard me... what?"

"Threaten to 'blow up the school'."

Matt stared at the detective, uncomprehending.

"Threaten to 'massacre' as many people as you could. In the school cafeteria today, just a few hours ago. Are you denying it?"

"Y-Yes! I'm denying it."

"You're denying it."

"I think this is all crazy."

"'This is all crazy.' That's your response?"

There was an undertone of disgust and incredulity in the man's voice that reminded Matt of his dad. Matt shivered.

On the table a tape recorder was running. The detectives were also taking notes. Mr Parrish had removed his glasses and was stroking his eyes as if they ached. There was a glimmer of perspiration on the principal's upper lip, and his face was crisscrossed with faint lines like scratches with a dry pen. His assistant was there, a young woman frowning over a notepad. Mrs Hale, the school guidance counsellor, and Mr

Rainey, the school psychologist, were present, staring at Matt as if they'd never seen him before.

It was then that Matt did an unexpected thing. He grinned.

His mouth twisted like some sort of rubber mouth. Maybe he even laughed. Mr Parrish said sharply, "Matthew, this isn't funny. Very serious accusations have been made against you."

"I'm not... I don't think it's funny," Matt said quickly.

He was feeling tired suddenly. As if he'd been running around the track for miles.

"Let's go over what we've been told. You did, or did not, make threats to 'blow up the school' in the cafeteria today?"

"Look, ask my friends! They can tell you."

"Certainly we will. If it's necessary, we will."

Matt had given them the guys' names: Russ, Skeet, Neil, Cal... Who else? But Mrs Hale said, "We don't want to involve anyone unless it's necessary. We'd like to clear this up at the source."

"Well, if I'm the source," Matt said, sarcastically, "I can tell you: I never threatened anybody or anything." His heart was beating hard. He recalled a story of Edgar Allan Poe's he'd read in Mr Weinberg's class last semester, *The Imp of the Perverse*. He said, his mouth twisting again, "And if I had, I wouldn't tell you, about it, would I?"

There was stunned silence. Mr Parrish's assistant shifted uneasily in her chair.

"Just a joke, officers," Mr Parrish said. His face was becoming mottled as if with hives. "Matthew means to be funny."

"Do you think this is 'funny', Matthew? Our conversation?"

"No, sir."

"We'd hoped to clear the air, Matthew. Without bringing you to headquarters."

"OK, I'm sorry. I didn't mean it."

"Didn't mean – what?"

"I didn't mean – the last thing I said."

"Which was—?"

They wanted him to speak into the tape recorder, that was it. Anything he said would be, will be, used against him in a court of law. Matt's mouth twitched. It *was* funny!

No, this was serious. Matt repeated what he'd said, and added an apology. The detective with the glasses was beginning to dislike him, he could tell. The other detective, younger and thicker bodied, regarded Matt with more sympathy. Or so Matt thought. "Now you're saying you are serious, you are telling the truth, yes? You're not lying now."

"Yes, sir. I mean – no."

"You're *not* lying now?"

"I wasn't l-lying, no. It was just a dumb joke."

"Do you consider a bomb threat, a threat to 'massacre' as many people as possible, a 'dumb joke'? Or something more serious?"

"Look, ask the other guys! They'll tell you."

"But why would they tell us, Matt, if you won't? If you're all involved in a conspiracy together?"

"We're not in any conspiracy, we're *not*. This is all crazy! It's exaggerated! I never said anything like that."

Mr Rainey said quietly, to Mr Parrish, maybe they should

contact the other boys now; and Mr Parrish said, in an undertone, he was hoping to avoid making an issue of this. "You know how upset parents in this district can get."

The questioning, the clearing of the air, continued. Matt had been thinking of it as a kind of TV sitcom in which he was the star, he'd have all the good lines (if he could only think of them), but it wasn't like that at all. The others, the adults, had the script; and he was floundering. He was stammering, he was fighting back tears. He couldn't stop his mouth from twisting, like a two-year-old on the verge of a tantrum. No, no! This was serious. He knew it was very serious. He'd clear the air, yes. He was an intelligent kid; Mr Weinberg praised him. Other teachers praised him. He'd explain to these adults in an assured, mature voice, and clear everything up. Maybe his mom and dad would not be contacted. (Matt wanted to think this so badly.) Maybe, if things got cleared quickly enough, he could return to study hall, and everybody would be relieved and happy to see him. Mr Weinberg would make one of his jokes – "Well, Matthew Donaghy! I see you made bail." Or – "I guess you're being recruited for the CIA, maybe?" And Matt would blush, and think of some witty response. Everybody would laugh.

He'd return to his desk, acting nonchalant. Stacey would be relieved. Maybe she'd squeeze his hand, in front of the others. "Oh, Matt! What was that all about?" Russ and Skeet would be dying to know, too. But Matt would tease his friends by taking out his play script and opening his laptop. In a mock-Brit accent he'd say, "Now, where were we when I was interrupted... ?"

He wanted to think this, so badly.

*I never said anything. I never meant anything.*
*Please won't anybody believe me?*

Out in the corridor a bell was ringing. Study period was over, for ever. It was like a plane you'd missed.

Never could Matt Donaghy return to that study hall. Never let the other kids see it was all a joke, it was nothing.

So strange: to hear the bell, to remain seated. With these adults. These strangers he feared and hated. While the other students were leaving classrooms, in a noisy herd on the stairs, rattling their lockers. He had a quick flash of Stacey, in tears. She was frightened for him! Or just embarrassed she knew him...

"Look, can I leave now? I told you everything I can tell you, over and over. I'm... expected at Drama Club."

"Not just yet, Matt. Maybe in a little while."

"When we clear this up, Matt. We have a few more things to clarify."

"But I've told you everything. I just keep repeating myself. Please, would you talk to my friends? There's Russ Mercer, there's 'Skeet' – Frank Curlew. There's Neil—"

*Please.* The word sounded so desperate, so cringing and begging, in Matt's mouth. He was feeling sick.

Mr Parrish assured Matt they would talk to his friends, soon. If it was necessary. Maybe it wouldn't be necessary.

Matt's spirits lifted a little, hearing this. Mr Parrish liked Matt, didn't he? He was a friendly principal, a "hands-on principal" he called himself, determined to maintain and to improve Rocky River's "tradition of high academic standards"

37

but hey, just a regular guy, eyeglasses winking at you in the hall, a wide quick smile asking, How's it going? He was an OK principal, a nice man, Matt believed, or wished to believe. *He's on my side. I'm a student here. He wants this cleared up more than I do.* Matt's mother came to PTA meetings and made it a point to speak with the principal, the guidance counsellor, the psychologist, Matt's track coach, all of Matt's teachers. These were people who would be writing letters of recommendation for Matt when he applied for college next year. Crucial to make a good impression on them! *Get them to like you. Get them on your side.*

The conversation continued. The clearing of the air.

The detectives asked to see the contents of Matt's backpack, and he showed them. He was sullen but cooperative. *An invasion of my privacy. Don't you need a warrant?* Next, as he'd known they would, they asked him to take them to his locker, to let them examine his locker, and at this Matt balked. "No, sir." Suddenly he was stubborn, he would not cooperate.

Mr Parrish asked him. The others. Concerned for him. Pretending not to be alarmed, suspicious.

But Matt shook his head no. His face was blazing hot.

Why? Because he was ashamed. Didn't want anybody to see the detectives going through his things.

His mouth twitched in an angry grin. "If you're expecting to find guns and bombs, I wouldn't be stupid enough to put them in my locker, would I?" He knew this was a mistake. But he couldn't seem to stop. "That's the first place somebody would look, isn't it?"

The detectives were staring at him.

"You tell us, son. You're the one who knows."

Sure, he knew they could open his locker, legally, without his permission. The principal of Rocky River High was the one to give, or withhold, permission. Mr Parrish might have waited for a search warrant, but he was eager to cooperate with police. "You won't find anything," Matt wanted to sneer at them. He wanted to laugh except he was too scared suddenly.

They found nothing. Which proved nothing.

They took Matt Donaghy to Rocky River police headquarters in an unmarked police vehicle. He wasn't handcuffed. He was accompanying the detectives "voluntarily". They'd allowed him to telephone his mother, and she would be joining them downtown.

Fortunately, Matt's father was away for another night.

"Matt, there isn't any" – his mother was blinking rapidly, wiping at her damp eyes – "truth to this charge, is there?"

"Mom! For God's sake, *no*."

They were alone together, briefly. At police headquarters. In a windowless fluorescent-lit room. On a Formica-topped table were Styrofoam cups with the dregs of coffee in them, an ugly black plastic ashtray heaped with cigarette ashes and butts. Matt hurriedly explained to his mother what had happened. What a misunderstanding it was. Just a joke, and he'd been overheard and misunderstood. Some "witnesses" – he didn't know who they were – were claiming he'd said something he hadn't. His mom wasn't absorbing much of this, wanting to embrace him, tears brimming in her eyes. "These – 'witnesses' – who are they? Why would they be spreading lies about you, Matt?"

To this question Matt had no answer.

It was a shock to him, to see his mother so agitated. And knowing he was to blame. His dad would never forgive him. He'd need to keep her at arm's length; the last thing he wanted to do was break down like a baby.

Wordlessly, he shook hands with Mr Leacock, "his" attorney.

And he shook hands with the middle-aged, kindly-faced female-from-Westchester-Family-Court, too.

"Matt Donaghy. I'm here to protect your rights."

All so crazy, like a dream. One of those exhausting dreams that go on and on. And maybe (Matt didn't want to think) it was just beginning.

Mr Leacock advised him to tell "all that you know" but to speak cautiously and never "incriminate" himself in any way. Matt was definitely not under arrest – yet – but it was urgent that the situation be resolved within a few hours so that everyone could go home.

So Matt told. Again.

He hadn't done anything wrong. He hadn't said anything wrong.

*Please* ask his friends to corroborate his story! Russ and Skeet and Neil and Cal and... he was forgetting who else had been there, at lunch... Denis Wheeler? They would clear Matt of all suspicion.

He tried not to speak sarcastically. He tried to hide the

rage he was feeling. Explaining to his silent audience (the detectives, the court-appointed female, his teary mother, and his attorney): why would he, of all people, want to blow up Rocky River High? He liked school. A lot. He liked his classes, and he liked lots of people, he'd been elected vice president of his class. And he'd never owned a gun, *never fired a gun*...

Matt began to stammer. He began to cough, and someone handed him a cup of water. He drank – the water was tepid. His hand was trembling. His eyes snatched at his mom's. They were both remembering how, at his uncle Jax's summer place in Jackson Hole, Wyoming, he'd fired a .22 rifle. This was a few years ago; Matt might've been thirteen. Uncle Jax had wanted to teach him, and Matt had wanted to be taught, it seemed a thing a guy would do, and talk about back east with his friends. What Matt mainly remembered about the rifle was its surprising weight, and the loud jarring *crack!* when he pulled the trigger. He'd never come anywhere near hitting a target.

He looked away from his mom. He didn't want to know what she was remembering, and what she might be thinking.


Who were the "witnesses" who'd gone to Mr Parrish's office to report Matt Donaghy?

Their identities were being protected at this time.

Mr Leacock objected that his client had a right to know who was accusing him.

Matt was saying again, patiently: whoever they were, they'd heard him wrong. Whatever they thought they'd heard, they'd gotten it wrong.

Or somebody was deliberately spreading lies to hurt him.

But why? Why hurt *him*?

When he was just... Matt Donaghy?

Sixteen. A junior at Rocky River High. A steady A-minus student (except for English, where he received mostly As). He wrote for the school paper and literary magazine, he'd been elected vice president of his class (by just eleven votes), people seemed to like him all right, he wasn't the best-looking guy at Rocky River but with his freckled face and quick smile he was OK, but there was a deeper seriousness, an edginess, he kept to himself. He wasn't weird. He wasn't a loner, a computer freak. He wasn't into sick stuff on the Internet like some guys. He'd had a lot of the same friends since grade school, and his friends were terrific. His teachers had always liked him....

Mr Weinberg would vouch for Matt. Mr Drewe, the boys' track coach, would vouch for him. *Not a star runner but a good team player.*

Suddenly it was like Matt was on trial.

No, Matt did not do drugs. And he didn't smoke. Maybe he had a few beers, sometimes. At parties.

Well, he smoked... sometimes. But not really. He wasn't stupid, he knew the health risk. He wasn't into tobacco, nicotine. He'd actually chewed a plug of tobacco not long ago, a friend gave him, and it was a totally disgusting experience. He'd swallowed some of the juice and gotten the sickest he'd ever been, trembling and vomiting. And the guys laughing at him. He didn't do drugs, either. Well, he'd tried some things. Everybody tried some things. He'd done "X", Ecstasy, but it made his heart race and left him breathless, made him paranoid, which was scary. No, he didn't hang out with a drug crowd. You heard of some of the older kids doing coke, heroin, but Matt wasn't in that crowd. What he was guilty of, he guessed, was saying stupid things. To make people laugh. He was sure, that day at lunch, when Skeet had teased him about maybe not being picked for the Arts Festival when it meant so much to him, he'd said something like, "What could I do, blow up the school?" and when that got a few laughs, he might have said, "Massacre a few hundred people?" and Skeet was into it, typical Skeet, pounding the table, laughing, as if the idea of Matt Donaghy doing such a thing was hilarious, "Like Columbine! *Viva* Columbine!" and Matt jumped to his feet making machine-gun-spraying gestures, in a crouch, pretending to be opening a coat, "Vroom-vroom-VROOM," and by this time all the guys at the table were into it, or most of them, Skeet, Russ, Cal, just showing off, wanting people to notice them. Girls at nearby tables, pretty girls like Stacey Flynn glancing over at them, smiling, with a look of *You guys! Grow up.* Or *What's so funny?* Indulging the guys as they'd been doing since first grade. But it was crowded in the cafeteria, and other people were passing by their table, which was in the centre aisle, and maybe somebody heard... or misheard. So if there was anything Matt Donaghy was guilty of, he supposed, it was acting dumb, juvenile. Lots of times like this he'd be ashamed afterwards. Because he wasn't like that really. He was a serious person really. He wanted to be a writer, a playwright. He wanted to perform in his own plays. That meant work, and brains, not goofing off like an asshole. The problem was, Matt had a talent for it: making people laugh. Even as a small kid he'd been mouthy, and funny. Adults had laughed at him. If people laughed, they liked being around you, it was a good feeling. They were apt to like *you*. Sure, Matt admired people who didn't seem to care if anybody liked them – Mr Jenkins, who taught calculus, for instance. And Mr Rainey, the school psychologist, who had to meet with parents who weren't happy that their children were having "psychological" problems. And there was that big girl with the fierce staring eyes: Ursula Riggs. A star girl athlete. Didn't seem to give a damn whether she was "well liked" or not. Maybe because her father was a big-shot CEO.... Matt was different. He needed to be special. Somehow. To make people like him. So he'd hear his mouth go on and on like it had a life of its own. Like he was a ventriloquist's dummy and didn't know what he was saying, sometimes. Saying things he didn't mean. Like on TV, the grossest stand-up comics saying things you aren't supposed to say, late-night cable... like to do with sex, race, people's bodies, going to the bathroom... school shootings, bombs. On TV you know it isn't real, it's just... comedy. A guy with a big mouth and a microphone. People laughing their heads off. Mr Weinberg warned: it's the violating of taboo, that's why people laugh. Sometimes they're shocked, and they laugh. But others will hate you and turn against you. So you have to be careful. Not that Matt was crude, much. He had a big mouth sometimes, but... how was that a crime? In the United States we have a Bill of Rights guaranteeing us freedom of speech and freedom of expression.

Don't we?

# six

"Ursula, what're you watching?"

It was the local news, WWRR. Six o'clock. There on TV was the buff-coloured brick facade of Rocky River High, and standing in front of it on the sidewalk, in a flurry of snowflakes, was a stylish female reporter with widened eyes and a microphone in her hand. "Rumours of a bomb threat and potential hostage taking at Rocky River High sometime this afternoon have not been confirmed, repeat: *not been confirmed* by either school authorities or Rocky River police." Cut to a fleeting vision of Mr Parrish, frowning and shaking his head – "No comment." The reporter identified this elusive figure as "Harold Parrish, Principal of Rocky River High, Westchester County. Mr Parrish is believed to have met with Rocky River police this afternoon, yet he denies reports of trouble at this highly regarded suburban school—" Disgusted, I switched to another channel. Here the news was about an actual bombing in the Mideast.

Too bad – my sister Lisa had seen. She said, "Was that your *school*? What's happening?"

"No. It's nothing."

"Why'd you turn it off? Turn it back, Ursula, c'mon!"

"*No*. I said it was nothing."

"She said 'Rocky River High' – I heard her."

Lisa tried to take the remote control from me, but I raised it over my head – which was far beyond my little sister's reach. When she tried to get to the TV to change the channel, I lifted her by the hips, as in a ballet move, and carried her out of the room.

Lisa batted at my hands, protesting. But she liked attention from me, her big Big Sis. Everybody in the family said Lisa "looked up to me" so I'd better be a good example for her, but I just laughed.

*Sure. Like Ugly Girl is a foot taller than Lisa, naturally the runt looks up to me.*

I was trying hard to stave off an Inky Black. Being depressed is *boring*. My knee was aching like hell, so I took three Tylenol as Ms Schultz recommended for "minor" aches and pains. The knee was swollen and turning an exotic shade of purple-gold, like a tropical sunset. My right wrist and forearm were bruised too.

*Ugly Girl, warrior.*

*So? You lose a few.*

Already the "news" was on TV. You'd really wonder what was going on at Rocky River High, the rumour was presented as so tantalising. Like Mr Parrish himself was involved in a cover-up. I was relieved that Matt Donaghy's name hadn't been mentioned. But it looked as if the rumour was correct – police had been at school. Everybody would be on the phone, or sending e-mails. Something was going on....

One good thing: nobody would give a damn about the girls' basketball team losing a game we should have won. Nobody would give a damn that Ursula Riggs had let the team down.

"I didn't! I didn't lose on purpose."

I shut the door to my room. I sat at my computer, and quick before I changed my mind, I sent an e-mail message to Ms Schultz.

Thurs 1/25/01 6:15 PM

dear ms schultz--
i am quitting the team. you know why.
UR

I thought this might keep away the Inky Black, but no, it possibly made things worse.

When Ms Schultz didn't e-mail me back that night, or next morning before school, it definitely made things worse.

*Ugly Girl. Family scene.*

"Ursula, I hope you understand. I wanted so badly to—"

"Sure, Mom."

" – Lisa and I, both—"

"It's OK, Mom."

"But by the time I picked her up from school—"

47

"Right, Mom. Cool."

Mom was watching me with her worried-mom/guilty-mom eyes. We were all in the kitchen preparing dinner. Since I'd become a vegetarian in ninth grade, I prepared most of my own food. I had my own work space in the kitchen, at the butcher-block table. Meat disgusted me, especially when it was raw. Actual living, *now dead* muscle tissue! My mom and dad weren't too happy that Lisa had become a vegetarian, too; she's real thin, with a skeletal structure like a sparrow's. Lisa and I were having tofu, soy sauce, green beans, mushrooms, chopped tomatoes and unsalted brown rice. Mom was preparing something gross for herself and Dad, but they wouldn't be eating until late, after Lisa and I were finished.

For a while I'd refused to sit at the same table with persons eating animal tissue. Until my dad said he was hurt. He wasn't home for dinner lots of nights, and when he was, where was Ursula? – upstairs in her room. So I relented. When Mom served fish or seafood, I'd eat with them. But at school I sat at a table by myself when Bonnie or Eveann were eating stuff with meat in it.

Because it was vegetables, rice, et cetera, I ate a lot of it. And yogurt, and nuts. And coarse brown bread. I drank a lot of fruit juice, especially grapefruit. I wasn't on any diet, for sure. Not Ugly Girl.

I had muscles, which you don't get from dieting.

Tonight in the kitchen Mom was saying, in this innocent voice, "Ursula, that looks good. Will you make a little extra for me, too?" I knew what she was doing but I said OK. I believed strongly in not eating meat and intended to convert the entire family, but I never said much about it because, if you do, people get defensive and say asshole cliché things. Like my own father, who's an intelligent man, telling me like it's some profound fact that carnivores are meant by nature to eat meat – "That's why we have the teeth we have."

Right off I'd say, "Teeth, Dad? A man your age wouldn't have teeth by now. If you're talking a state of 'nature' you'd be gumming soft mushy stuff like tofu."

Which made Dad wince. Of all the foods in existence, it's tofu that really turns him off.

I said, "The actual truth is, Dad, just a hundred years ago a man your age would maybe not be alive. The other day in biology I saw this chart, the average life expectancy for men wasn't much over forty. And the cholesterol and stuff from animal fat would be blocking your arteries, and you wouldn't have a clue what was happening."

Dad shuddered and said, OK, he got my point.

I overheard Dad saying to Mom, in this voice like he was, in spite of himself, impressed, "Our older daughter is quite an idealist, isn't she?" And Mom said, in this voice I couldn't interpret, "She needs it, Clay. Let's just hope it lasts."

I resented that! I didn't understand it but I resented it.

Sometimes I hated Mom. I hated her looking at me, and thinking her thoughts about me. Ugly Girl scorned the eyes of others, but if it's your own mother looking at you close up, those eyes are hard to ignore.

Now Mom was smiling this forced little guilty smile. "Ursula, you haven't said a word about the game. I hope—"

"We lost. That's two words."

"Oh, Ursula. But was it – a good game?"

I shrugged. I was spooning rice on to plates. Ordinarily by this time of evening after a game or practice I'd be famished, but tonight, the Inky Black creeping up on me like oil ooze, I felt funny. Not just because I was ashamed and angry about the game, but the rumour about Matt Donaghy was sort of sickening, too. The way, talking with those people at school, Ugly Girl who should've been superior to a lynch mob had kind of grooved with it at first, like the others.

*Liking it that somebody else was in trouble.*

"*I* wanted to see you play, Ursula," Lisa said.

I shrugged. I was pissed at Lisa, too. Evidently.

My mother and sister exchanged a glance. Thinking I wouldn't notice.

Lisa was eleven, I was sixteen. When she was born I was five years old. I'd always been The Baby in the Riggs family, and it was a shock to discover that there's a place for only one of these in a family. Lisa was The Baby from that day onwards, and what Ursula was I didn't know.

I mean, eventually I knew. But not for a long time.

Mom began again with some excuse, as if she hadn't missed most of my games this season, and I said, "Mom, you didn't miss a thing. Don't *obsess.*"

"Well, I hope you enjoyed the game, at least."

"'Enjoy'? Losing?"

"You know what I mean, honey. Sports aren't just about winning, I thought."

I knew Mom was right. This was my philosophy too. But I said nothing.

Mom never missed driving Lisa to dance lessons. And staying for the lessons, lots of times. Over the holiday break she'd taken Lisa to see the New York City Ballet twice. Of course, I'd been invited to join them.

Did I mind that Lisa was everybody's favourite? Truthfully I did not. I couldn't stand prissy little ballerinas – the word "ballerina" made my lip curl – and prissy dance music like *The Nutcracker* and *Swan Lake* made me want to puke, but if other people adored it, fine. Girls with collarbones and pelvic bones poking through their leotards gliding and spiralling and leaping, trying not to grimace in agony when their toes are being crushed *en pointe* against a hardwood floor – fine. Anorexic eleven-year-olds – fine. Mom liked to tell us how she'd taken ballet lessons as a little girl, too. Mom was small boned, the kind of woman who likes to be told she's petite. Like it's a compliment. My Ugly Girl genes I obviously inherited from Dad.

We were carrying dishes into the dining room. I must have limped a little, because Mom was on me like a hawk. "Ursula, were you hurt in that game?"

"I'm fine, Mom."

"Is it your knee?"

"No."

"Oh, Ursula." Mom touched my hair, and I shrank from her. She pulled up my sleeve, and I almost shoved her away. "Are those bruises, Ursula?"

"Nope."

"What are they, then?"

"Dirt."

This made Lisa giggle. I laughed too. Ugly Girl had a loud harsh laugh that didn't invite you to join in.

Mom started fussing over me. I said, "I'm going to eat in my room. I've got a lot of reading to do for tomorrow."

"Ursula, you are not going to eat in your room. You're going to eat with us."

"You're not eating, are you?"

"I am. I'll sit with you. Please."

"'Please' – what?"

"Don't be rude, Ursula. I'm very tired, and—"

"Mom, what's 'rude' about having a lot of homework to do? It's Civil War history. *I* didn't choose it."

Lisa giggled again. Mom was staring at me with these tragic eyes that looked watery and not-young. "Ursula, I told you I was sorry about missing your game, but my schedule is so – complicated. With your father away so much, and maintaining this house, my life—"

I hated Mom talking this way. Especially in front of Lisa. You don't want your mom to plead with you. I remembered hearing this sound in her voice, like a stricken bird, last summer in Nantucket. We have a big old white-shingled house there on the water and Dad flies up on Thursdays and stays till Sunday evenings in August. This time I was thinking of, Dad had just arrived from the airport, and he and Mom were together in their bedroom and the door was shut and *I wasn't listening* but I heard the voices, something in her voice, the pleading sound, abject and yet coercive, and Dad's deeper voice, meant to reassure. I was so scared suddenly. *Don't leave us, Dad. Not yet. Daddy, please.*

Bonnie LeMoyne's father left them, two years ago. Bonnie swallowed twenty capsules of her mother's barbiturates and called me on the phone and I came over and made her puke the mess up into the toilet. Chalky-white glop and Diet Pepsi that, I swear, still had some fizzle. That was Bonnie and Ugly Girl's secret together – no one else knew.

Ugly Girl would never overdose on barbiturates. Or Diet Pepsi.

If Ugly Girl did, you can be sure she'd never lose her courage and telephone a friend.

I gave in and ate downstairs. Lisa lit candles on the dining-room table. Mom sat with us, picking at her tofu and rice and saying how delicious it was. She'd poured a glass of wine and was sipping it slowly. Dad was expected home, she said, around eight – or eight thirty – but who knew? He might call, or might not. It was Dad's schedule, his life that was complicated; Mom's life was just busy.

I'd made Lisa promise not to say anything to Mom about the TV news, and I was surprised – Lisa kept her promise. Or maybe she'd just forgotten? I knew Mom would find out soon, and I didn't want to talk about it with her. While we were eating, I mentioned maybe I'd be quitting the basketball team, and both Lisa and Mom reacted with disappointment. "Oh, Ursula!" Lisa said. "Don't quit, you're so *good*."

My kid sister's eyes were so beautiful, warm and dark and fine-lashed like a doll's eyes, that sometimes it was hard for Ugly Girl to be jealous of her.

"Ursula! Come here!"

Mom called me downstairs. It was the ten o'clock news, another station. This time a male broadcaster with a toupee like a flat black pancake fixed over his head was saying gravely that Rocky River police were "not yet releasing the identity of a Rocky River High School student who allegedly threatened to bomb the school and massacre hundreds of his fellow classmates and teachers". Cut to a very harassed-looking Mr Parrish backing away, amid snow flurries, from an aggressive reporter shoving a microphone into his face. Mr Parrish said, with as much dignity as he could muster, "I said – I have no comment at this time." Cut to a Rocky River plainclothes detective frowning into the camera. "The alleged incident is being investigated. No, no arrests have been made." Cut to the broadcaster in his studio, with an insert of the facade of Rocky River High in the lower left-hand corner of the screen. "It's believed that a fifteen-year-old student at the high school has been suspended from classes pending a thorough investigation. At the present time it isn't known if the boy has a juvenile record or a psychiatric history or even if he was conspiring with others in the alleged plot. And now—" Cut to Manhattan, the facade of City Hall.

"This is so wrong. My God, this is so *crazy*, and so *wrong*."

Mom was all agitated, as I knew she'd be. Asking if I knew about this. If the school had been "evacuated". I told her it was nothing but a rumour. "Then you know about it, Ursula?"

"No! I mean – I know about the rumour."

"How do you know it's only a rumour?"

*Because I was there, I was a witness.*

I ran my hands through my hair, leaving it spiky. Lisa was still up, in her pyjamas, staring at me wide-eyed. Dad hadn't come home yet, evidently. I hoped for Mom's sake that he'd called in, but I didn't remember hearing the phone ring. I started back upstairs, and Mom called after me, "Ursula! What do you know about this? Do you know the boy?"

It was too complicated to get into with Mom. She'd been drinking, I could tell. Her skin flushed and a look about her lower face like it was soft bread dough, sagging.

I shut the door to my room and locked it. Mom followed me and knocked on the door. "Ursula? What are you doing? Please—" I knew after a few minutes she'd get discouraged, if I didn't fall into the trap of exchanging shouts with her through the door.

I was trembling, the TV news had made me so pissed. Not a bit of it was true – I'd heard exactly what Matt Donaghy had said in the cafeteria, and I'd seen what he'd done. It must be a nightmare for him, I thought.

I wanted to call him but had trouble finding the right Donaghys in the phone book. I didn't know his father's name or where they lived. At the first number I called, there was a busy signal. The phone must've been off the hook. The next number I called, a surly character answered – "If this is another goddamned reporter, you have the *wrong number*." The receiver was slammed down hard.

I tried the last two Donaghys and got only answering machines. I hung up.

Sure, I knew this was "impulsive" behaviour. My mom – and also my dad – were always warning me not to behave "impulsively". But I knew what I had to do, and I was going to do it, which is Ugly Girl's way, so I looked up Russ Mercer's phone number in the directory, and called him, and the phone just rang; and I looked up Cal Carter, and no luck. It was like Matt Donaghy's friends had all disappeared. I hated that guy Skeet – squirmy, smirky little creep who rolled his eyes at girls when he thought they couldn't see and, behind Ugly Girl's back (so the jerk thought), made lewd female-figure gestures with his hands. So I couldn't call Skeet, for sure. But I got along really well with Matt's friend Denis Wheeler, who was in my biology class, so I called Denis, and thank God he answered, sounding nervous, and he didn't want to talk about Matt (like he'd been warned against it, by his parents maybe?) but he was nice enough to give me Matt's e-mail address so I e-mailed this message:

Thurs 1/25/01 10:23 PM

dear matt--
please call me, its urgent.

your classmate URSULA RIGGS

I left my number and at ten forty-seven P.M. the phone rang.

# SEVEN

**Ursula Riggs! This** had to be a joke.

One of Matt's friends, pretending to be URSULA RIGGS.

None of the guys he'd e-mailed had answered him yet. Not one.

Maybe this was Skeet's way of answering? Skeet had a weird sense of humour, sometimes cruel.... On this nightmare day, Matt figured anything could happen to him. He'd never even been told who his accusers were. He'd been suspended from school for "at least three days, pending a thorough investigation".

Like Matt had AIDS. Some kind of airborne AIDS that was contagious by just being in the same room with one so afflicted.

Matt's mother and Mr Leacock had protested. But Mr Parrish's decision was final. A three-day suspension – minimum. *But my son has done nothing wrong. Not a thing wrong!* Pending a thorough investigation. *But Matthew is the one who's been wronged. This is so unfair!*

Hearing he'd been suspended, Matt had come close to bursting into tears.

Police would sift through "evidence". Matt Donaghy's academic and personal files at Rocky River High. His IQ score. (What was Matt's IQ? Somewhere around 135. There were brainy kids at Rocky River whose IQs were way beyond that.) His "psychological" profile. They would interview his teachers, and his friends. They would interview classmates who weren't his friends. They would examine his satirical-humour columns for the student newspaper, and they had in their possession (Matt had given them a copy, disgusted) the play manuscript *William Wilson: A Case of Mistaken Identity.* Matt winced to think of strangers reading his silly, sophomoric sketch, highlighting with Magic Markers the passages that were "violent".

And if they read the Edgar Allan Poe story, they would think – what? This kid is psychotic. This kid is really, really sick.

At the police station Matt came to understand why a person in custody, though innocent, suddenly "confesses".

He understood why a person in custody, in the presence of police officers he knows to be armed, suddenly goes crazy and starts to fight them.

Or runs from them. Like a panicked animal, desperate to escape.

Even with his mother present, and his attorney, and the well-intentioned woman from Family Court, Matt had come close to breaking down in the interrogation room. Shouting in their faces – "Yes! I do want to murder you all." Attacking the detective who was asking most of the questions, trying to strangle him, trying to wrestle his gun away from him. Like a movie scene it would be, so fast, and Matt would manage to shoot the bastard even as he was himself shot, riddled with bullets. Dying in a pool of warm blood on the dirty floor.

Anything to escape their questions. To say *No more!*

Instead, he'd jammed his fingers against his mouth to keep from crying.

He'd halfway thought, at first, back at the high school, that this was some wild comical adventure he could write about for the paper, and entertain his friends with. Girls would be impressed, wide-eyed. But now he knew: they'd never understand.

He would never be able to express to another person the weakness he was feeling, and the rage.

At home, he'd quickly e-mailed Russ, Skeet, Cal and Neil. And not one of them had answered.

He'd e-mailed Russ and Skeet a second time.

Hey guys: where're you hiding?
You can come out. All clear.

And, to Russ, a third time.

Russ, it's OK. I mean, I think it is.
Could you call? Thanks!

But Russ hadn't answered.

(At least not yet.)

And now there glimmered on his computer screen this message from URSULA RIGGS that was possibly a joke?

If it was a joke of Skeet's, the number would be Ursula's actual number. Leave it to Skeet to see to details like that.

He couldn't take a chance, though. Couldn't call her.

Ursula Riggs. It would be ironic if, out of the whole school, of Matt's numerous friends and acquaintances and classmates, only Ursula Riggs, whom he scarcely knew, was contacting him.

But no. It was Skeet.

Had to be Skeet...

"Damn you, Skeet."

Matt resented it that Skeet wasn't in trouble too. Skeet had been the one to egg Matt on. If Skeet hadn't been there in the cafeteria, and the other guys looking to Matt for laughs, none of this crap would have happened.

It was like, that time when Matt was twelve, he'd dived from a high board at the community pool without knowing what the hell he was doing, only that the guys were there grinning up at him, and Matt was clowning around for them as usual. He'd struck the surface of the water with a *slap* that left his chest and belly raw-red afterwards, and somehow his nose was bleeding. He'd smacked his nose against his knees?

Even after they saw Matt's nose bleeding, the guys laughed.

And another time, doing a handstand on a step, a marble step in a flight of stairs at the Museum of Natural History in Manhattan, where their eighth-grade science class had been taken on a field trip. Crazy! Matt might have broken his neck, his back. Might be in a wheelchair for life.

Would the guys want to have lunch with him in the cafeteria, in his wheelchair? Would they come visit him at home?

Or that summer he'd turned into a skateboard freak. Gliding in and out of traffic near the mall until a cop caught him and gave him hell and brought him home to his mom. He'd been fourteen, and knew better. And he couldn't blame any of the guys for that.

"You could be killed, Matt!" Mom cried reproachfully. "Don't you *care*?"

Maybe he hadn't. Or maybe he'd needed to impress his friends.

Now Matt's dog, Pumpkin, a golden retriever, was nudging her head, her damp cold nose, against Matt's hands. She knew. She knew something was wrong. She worried when Matt didn't come directly home from school, and today he'd been gone for hours. She'd heard Matt on the phone with his dad for an hour and forty minutes. Before that she'd heard the raised voices as they'd come into the house from the garage, Matt and his mom.

Pumpkin had heard Matt's brother, Alex, asking in a scared voice what was wrong. Alex had been alone and had turned on the news... "What's going on at your school, Matt? Is this guy somebody you know?" Alex had looked both frightened and excited, and Matt had shouted at him, "Fucking *no*. Fucking mind your own *business*."

Mom was on him then for that, using "the f word" in her hearing.

And for shouting at his brother – "Matt, you should be ashamed. You of all people."

What did that mean?

*You of all people. We expect better of you, Matt.*

Next, Matt had to speak with his father on the phone. It couldn't be avoided. Dad was in a hotel in Atlanta; he'd been scheduled to fly home that evening, but his flight was cancelled due to bad weather. Dad tried to speak calmly to Matt, but Matt could tell he was distraught, anxious.

Matt noted how his dad, just like his mom, began by asking, in a voice like a tight-strung wire, "Is there – any truth to this charge, Matt?"

Matt said flatly, "No."

Of course, they had to ask. It was a natural instinct.

Matt sat hunched on his bed. Listening to Dad's voice, and trying to answer Dad's rapid-fire questions. Thank God for Pumpkin. He could bury his warm face in her fur. Dad kept wanting to know if his name – "our name" – was in the news yet, and Matt said no, he didn't think so. "You're a minor. There's a law, I think. They can't release a minor's name. I think." Dad sounded as if he was thinking aloud. ". . . what a time for this to happen! I haven't told you and Alex but... I'm in a kind of transitional phase with the company. They're downsizing my department, and..."

Matt wanted to shove the phone receiver from him. No! He couldn't bear to hear this. He only half heard, as Dad talked in a rambling, incoherent way. (Had he been drinking? Maybe.) Away in the Four Seasons Hotel in Atlanta he was alternately dazed, angry, disbelieving, optimistic. "Don't worry, Matt. You're the wronged party here. We'll see that justice is done."

Sure, Dad.

There was an awkward pause before they hung up. Matt thought his father was going to ask him again if there was "any truth" to the charge, but finally Dad said, embarrassed, "Hey. I love you. You and Alex, my big guys. You know that, right?"

Matt mumbled, "Yeah. Thanks, Dad."


"Hey Pumpkin. *You* know I'm not a psycho, don't you?"

Pumpkin, rescued from an animal shelter when she was six weeks old, was now seven years old, with a thick torso but a beautiful wavy golden-russet coat and a dog's sympathetic dark-brown shiny eyes; she snuggled against Matt and assured him: She knew.

Even if Matt was a psycho, Pumpkin loved him anyway.

Pumpkin had been Matt's dog from the start. He'd promised his parents that he would housebreak her and train her, and he had. (His parents were impressed.) To Matt, Pumpkin would always be a puppy rolling over on her back in an ecstasy of being tickled by Matt alone.

"What do you think, Pumpkin? This 'URSULA RIGGS' – is it a joke, or real?"

Pumpkin's tail thumped tentatively. *She'd* give it a try, sure!

One thing Matt loved about Pumpkin: she was optimistic.

*Please call me, its urgent.*

It had to be about the trouble Matt was in, of course. Maybe Ursula Riggs was one of the anonymous "witnesses" who'd reported him to Mr Parrish? But no: not Ursula. That

63

big-boned brash girl with flyaway dark-blonde hair and studs in her ears like chips of broken glass and the soiled Mets cap on her head and the frank insolent blue-eyed stare. If you looked at Big Ursula, Big Ursula looked at you right back. She'd stare down any guy, or guys. Matt had to admire a girl like Ursula, though she made him uneasy, self-conscious.

No. Ursula wouldn't report anyone to any authorities; she was an anarchist by nature. Matt knew: he'd have liked to be an anarchist himself.

Instead he'd been a good boy. Dutiful, polite, only just pretending to be rebellious with his "humour". His instinct was to brownnose any adult in authority. And where had it gotten him? Suspended for three days. Minimum.

Twice Matt dialled the number Ursula had given him and twice he hung up quickly before the phone could ring. So damned shy. The third time he dialled, he let the phone ring and it was answered at once. "Hello?" The girl's voice was husky, guarded.

"Hi, this is... Matt. Is this Ursula?"

"Yes."

"I... got your message."

Matt was speaking in a lowered, shaky voice. He was feeling a leap of irrational hope.

Ursula said, still guardedly, "You know me, I guess? From school?"

"Ursula, sure. Sure I know you."

As if they hadn't been going to the same schools most of their lives.

Ursula said, "This hasn't been such a... great day for you, I guess."

"No. But—" Matt paused. He wanted to say, *At least I'm home, not in jail.* But that wasn't much of a reason to be grateful, considering he hadn't done anything wrong. " – I'm alive, anyway."

Was that meant to be funny? Matt laughed, but Ursula remained silent.

Matt had begun to sweat, this conversation was so pained. He hated calling girls on the phone if he didn't know them really well and if it hadn't been understood, more or less, that he was going to call, and was expected. He was even uneasy sometimes calling his friends. Which was why he liked e-mail. Maybe Ursula Riggs was the same way? Her telephone voice was unexpectedly hesitant, diffident.

Or maybe she just didn't like Matt Donaghy personally. But had to talk to him for some mysterious reason.

Ursula began speaking rapidly, as if her words were prepared. "Look, Matt. I heard what you said in the cafeteria today. I was walking past your table, and I heard. I know you were joking, and there's no way any intelligent person could misconstrue your words or gestures. If it's taken out of context, maybe, but there was a context. And I can be a witness for you. I'll go to Mr Parrish first thing tomorrow and talk to him. Or the police, if necessary."

By the end of this speech, Ursula was speaking vehemently. Matt wasn't sure he'd heard right. Witness? He felt like a drowning swimmer whose flailing hand has been grabbed by someone, a stranger, whose face he can't see.

He said, stammering, "You... heard me? You know I didn't... wasn't..."

"A friend of mine, Eveann McDowd, was with me. She heard you too. I'll talk to her."

"You'd – be a witness for me, Ursula? Gosh."

Ursula said quickly, "You've been falsely accused. I'd do it for anybody." She added, "I mean – even somebody I didn't like."

Matt was too confused to absorb what Ursula Riggs seemed to be saying. That she liked *him*? All he could say was to repeat, "Thanks, Ursula. I – really appreciate it.

"You're the only person who's contacted me, Ursula," Matt added impulsively. "I'm a pariah, I guess – is that the word? Like leper. Outcast." When Ursula didn't reply, Matt said, "I've been suspended for 'at least three days'. Till they can investigate me."

"Investigate *you*? They're the ones who should be investigated."

Ursula Riggs spoke so heatedly, it was as if, suddenly, she was in Matt's room with him and Pumpkin.

# Eight

**Friday morning, I** was desperate to leave for school as soon as possible, before Mom could stop me and make one of her Earnest Mom Appeals. But there she was, blocking my way.

And we go:

"Ursula! You are *not* going to get involved in this... situation at your school. Just because you happen to have overheard a few words you might have misunderstood. Your father and I both feel—"

That was Mom's way. Trying to cast doubt on what I knew to be absolutely true.

"—it would be a terrible mistake."

Ugly Girl inquired politely, "Whose mistake, Mom? Mine, or yours?"

"Ursula, this isn't funny."

Ugly Girl stood grave and attentive.

"It's just like you to get involved with a boy who's been

publicly accused of plotting to blow up your school, a boy we don't even know—"

Ugly Girl let this pass. Don't even know?

"—it will reflect upon *you*."

(And upon *you*?)

"Ursula, aren't you listening? I've been awake all night worrying – what if you're questioned too? As a – a co-conspirator? This could be a nightmare. It might get in the news. And if it gets put in your record—"

So that's where this was going. Sure. Everything was risky, it could wind up in your record.

"—it will jeopardise your college application. You know how competitive the Ivy League schools are. Reckless behaviour now might ruin your entire life."

All right, Ugly Girl made a mistake. I'd told my mom what I'd heard in the cafeteria, and she'd told Dad. Evidently. I'd thought for sure they would want me to speak up for the truth.

But Mom had worked herself up into a state by now. It was like her to take one small thing and exaggerate it while neglecting everything else. Ugly Girl wanted to scream but bit her lower lip instead. One of Ugly Girl's principles was: Do Not Quarrel With the Enemy Unless Cornered. Mom was winding up by saying that she and Dad had "only your best interests at heart, honey"; in fact, she and Dad had been "up half the night, discussing this". They did not want me to speak with Mr Parrish this morning – "For your own good, Ursula. You're much too impetuous and careless. This is your life, and not just some... whim."

Whim! As if Ugly Girl's principles were based upon *whim*.

Calmly, Ugly Girl said, "Right. It's my life, Mom. Not yours or Dad's."

Friday morning, an hour later, at school:

Wild! Ugly Girl could see Mr Parrish start to squirm. His eyeglasses winking nervously, and his doughy face darkening with blood.

This was a morning very different from the previous afternoon in the gym. Ugly Girl was at her sharpest. Her most compelling and articulate. You would never guess she'd botched two foul shots and lost a game for Rocky River before a resentful, angry crowd. Of course, her opponent, a middle-aged high school principal, presented nothing like the competition of the canny Tarrytown team.

Ugly Girl was facing Mr Parrish across his big glass-topped desk (as if being principal of Rocky River High was such a big deal) with her spine ramrod straight, which made her appear a little taller than she actually was, and Ugly Girl was no runt. She was wearing her glittery ear studs, and her maroon satin school jacket with her gold school letter, and her khakis, and her faux palomino-hide boots; she'd removed the soiled Mets cap, of course, out of courtesy. Unflinchingly she fixed her steely blue eyes on the man's drawn face.

Ugly Girl was explaining to Mr Parrish that she'd been passing by Matt Donaghy's table at lunch the previous day, and she'd heard every word he'd said, and his friends' responses, and it was obvious – "Even a moron would understand, Mr Parrish" – that Matt was joking.

"But, Ursula, how could you be certain? If—"

"Mr Parrish, this friend of Matt's, Skeet Curlew, asked Matt what he'd do if his play wasn't chosen for the Festival, and Matt said, 'What could I do, blow up the school? Massacre some people?' The implication was that Matt *could not – would not* – do such a thing. No one in a million years would interpret it any other way."

Mr Parrish sighed, staring at Ugly Girl.

She said, patiently, "If you analyse Matt's remark, he was actually saying the opposite of what he's been accused of saying by these 'witnesses'. Sure, the guys were clowning pretending to be shooting guns; you know how guys that age are: immature. But everybody was laughing. It was a joke."

Parrish removed his glasses, rubbed his tired eyes, and replaced the glasses. Ugly Girl perceived that he believed her.

"*I* didn't laugh," Ugly Girl said, "because guys' humour doesn't turn me on. It's gross, it's dumb, but it isn't a national emergency or anything."

"Ursula, you are absolutely certain that you heard what you've just told me? *Absolutely certain?*"

"Absolutely, Mr Parrish."

"I'd hoped that someone... uninvolved with the boys would come forwards, before this got out of hand."

"A friend of mine was with me, Eveann McDowd, who will corroborate what I've said."

I wasn't sure of this. But Ugly Girl could try.

"Eveann McDowd." Mr Parrish noted this on a memo pad. "Very good. It's a relief to hear what you've said, Ursula. I want to thank you for coming forwards. Still, the investigation will have to be continued..."

"No!"

Mr Parrish looked at Ugly Girl in faint disbelief. Had this girl really said *No* to him, principal of Rocky River High?

Ugly Girl said, "I'd be worried, Mr Parrish, if I were *you*. You might be liable for suspending Matt Donaghy without probable cause, and defaming his character."

At this, Mr Parrish's doughy face grew even darker. "No one has defamed that boy's character. His name has not been released. We've been very careful."

"But everyone knows, Mr Parrish. It's an open secret."

"Naturally there's gossip. And the media is just as bad as everyone says. We can't help that. But..."

"But you do believe me? *You* do?"

Mr Parrish said, thoughtfully, "Yes, Ursula. Personally, I do. What you've said does sound... convincing. It's almost exactly what Matt has been insisting he said. We've questioned his friends, and they tell the same story, generally. Matt's teachers say he does a lot of joking, he's immature for his age, sometimes. But he's a very good student and everyone likes him." Mr Parrish paused, and here Ugly Girl could see the Earnest Principal Appeal approaching. "The reports brought to me, however, were serious. Very serious. I felt I had to call the police, not try to handle it myself."

Ugly Girl said, disgusted, "None of it was handled right! Lots of people are thinking – and saying – that Matt Donaghy really did something wrong. They're saying he's been arrested and questioned by the police. It's on TV and in the papers that there's a police investigation going on, like there is after an actual crime. You caused this by overreacting, Mr Parrish."

Mr Parrish said sarcastically, "You're a friend of this boy's, I take it?"

"I am not. I don't know him except by name."

"Look, we had to take into consideration the safety of every student and teacher in this building. We had to act swiftly. With school shootings in Colorado, Kentucky, Washington, and bomb scares, and threats, we had no way of knowing—"

"These 'witnesses' who accused Matt – who are they?"

Mr Parrish frowned. You could see he'd been asked this question many times and was finding it difficult to repeat the same words.

"They have asked that their identities remain anonymous. For their own protection."

"If there's a lawsuit," Ugly Girl said shrewdly, "their identities will be revealed. Fast."

"A – lawsuit?"

This hit a nerve. Ugly Girl knew.

She said, "If this goes on any longer. If Matt Donaghy isn't reinstated, and the whole thing called off. And publicly explained."

Perspiration gleamed on Mr Parrish's soft upper lip, and his forehead furrowed like a haphazardly ploughed field. At last he was losing his composure. "Ursula. Miss Riggs. Even if what you say is one hundred per cent true, and there's another girl to verify it, we had no way of knowing, yesterday afternoon, that—"

"Well, now you know, Mr Parrish."

And Ugly Girl stood, with dignity. And walked out of the principal's office without a backwards glance to see how he was staring after her.

Friday morning, later:

Eveann McDowd was saying in her weak, apologetic voice, "Ursula, gosh, I'd like to help him out. But I just can't. My mom doesn't want me to get involved, you know? I told her about yesterday, and how it's all exaggerated on TV and Matt Donaghy is innocent, and she says I'll be called a 'terrorist' too. On TV this morning there was something about a 'conspiracy of students' planning to blow up—"

Ugly Girl said severely, "Eveann, that's just crazy. And you know it."

"Sure, but—"

"*You* know it. Where's your conscience?"

Eveann looked at Ugly Girl shyly. She was a strange, unpredictable girl: sometimes as outspoken as Ugly Girl herself, but at other times uncertain, hesitant. Ugly Girl was always dropping Eveann as a friend, then taking her up again. This had been going on since sixth grade. "Ursula, I told you. I would talk to Mr Parrish... except for my mom."

Ugly Girl said, "I'll call your mom. Right now."

"Oh, Ursula! Maybe that isn't a good idea—"

It was eleven o'clock. Mrs McDowd was sure to be home. Though Eveann protested weakly, Ugly Girl marched into the front office to make the call, insisting she needed to use a phone, it was very important, related to the Matt Donaghy investigation. She called Eveann's mother and explained the situation to her, politely but emphatically. Ugly Girl knew that Mrs McDowd was a devout Catholic, so she figured Mrs McDowd must have a conscience too. "If Matt Donaghy gets into serious trouble, his life might be ruined. And anyone who knows he's innocent, and has been falsely accused, and doesn't speak up for him, will be morally guilty. We have to 'bear witness' for one another, Mrs McDowd. That's our Christian duty."

After a few minutes' conversation, Ugly Girl signalled for Eveann, who was close by biting her nails, to come talk to her mother. Ugly Girl was smiling, and almost immediately Eveann was smiling, too.

"Mom? Oh, thanks. I *will*."

I was feeling so good by the end of classes on Friday, the Inky Black mood evaporated like polluted air when the wind sweeps in from the Atlantic. Almost, I hadn't had time to think Ms Schultz never e-mailed me back asking me not to quit the team.

# NINE

"**Matt! Good News!** Pick up the phone."

On Monday, the second day of Matt Donaghy's suspension from Rocky River High, Matt's mother called excitedly to him, as he and Pumpkin entered the house at about three thirty P.M.

Matt had just returned from a snow-blown two-hour hike in the Rocky River Nature Preserve, with Pumpkin trotting and panting at his heels. It was weird – kind of exhilarating, but definitely weird – to be out tramping alone in the preserve when everybody else was in school. But Matt had needed to get out of the house, badly. He hadn't slept much since the previous Thursday, and his thoughts were coming rushed and confused like those strange thoughts you sometimes have on the verge of sleep; he'd shake his head to wake up, and then he was too much awake. *Suspended for three days. Minimum. Pending investigation.* He didn't want to think what might be happening, or not happening, at the high school. If Ursula Riggs and her friend had testified on his behalf. (He was sure they had, if Ursula said so.) If the guys had testified on his behalf. (He was sure they had. Though, still, over the long weekend, not one had e-mailed or called Matt.) He still hadn't been informed who his accusers were. (It was generally known that there were two of them, and they were in some way "related". Meaning what?) Mr Weinberg had e-mailed him a terse, thoughtful note on Friday morning:

This will be cleared up, Matt.
Use the unexpected free time to READ WRITE BROOD
DREAM.

Ursula Riggs had also e-mailed him a terse, hopeful note on Friday afternoon:

dear matt,
i spoke w/ principal perish this AM
eveann spoke w/ him this PM
FINGERS CROSSED FOR JUSTICE
                                    UR

"My two friends. And you, Pumpkin."

Matt was hugging Pumpkin a lot lately. He hadn't had so much time for Pumpkin since he'd been sick with the flu two years before.

•   •   •

It was a long weekend.

It was a long Monday morning waiting for a call that might not come. (Mr Leacock was "negotiating". Matt's parents had insisted that Matt be spared as much distress as possible.)

Sure, Matt tried to use the "free time" profitably. He'd tried to work ahead in his classes, and to rewrite *William Wilson: A Case of Mistaken Identity*, but the play just seemed childish to him now, like something he'd written in middle school. Matt wasn't even sure he understood the story by Edgar Allan Poe, which he'd reread. (There were two William Wilsons. Except there was just one William Wilson. Do they both die at the end?) Anyway, what was happening in his own life was like a play. A dark, nasty comedy where people's misery was held up to ridicule.

Matt's parents tried to shield him, and Alex, from what was being published in local papers. But Matt was too shrewd – he'd seen the headlines:

**WESTCHESTER COUNTY YOUTH SUSPENDED FROM SCHOOL**
Alleged Threat of Violence Investigated by Police

*– Westchester Journal*

**ROCKY RIVER H.S. STUDENT SUSPENDED PENDING INVESTIGATION**
Threats of Violence Not Tolerated, Warns Principal Parrish

*– Rocky River Gazette*

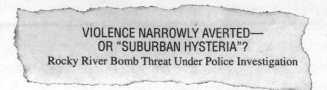

VIOLENCE NARROWLY AVERTED—
OR "SUBURBAN HYSTERIA"?
Rocky River Bomb Threat Under Police Investigation

– *The New York Times* (Metro Section)

The only good thing, Matt's father said, was that, so far, the name "Donaghy" hadn't been printed or spoken on TV or radio.

Matt didn't want to point out to him that everybody he, Matt, knew, knew. And those were all the people Matt cared about.

He'd hiked, hiked, hiked in the preserve until Pumpkin showed signs of faltering. Must've gone two or three miles in one direction, then circled back home. It was a bleak January sky like tarnish. The kind of day you'd never believe there could be spring. Matt was thinking, *I could run away! So easy.* There'd been a documentary on TV about runaway teenagers in San Francisco. Thousands of runaways a year, and their parents looking for them. (Maybe they weren't all looking very hard.) Climbing into, then up, a ravine strewn with icy rocks, he'd lost his footing and almost fallen. *So easy. Crack my head. No more misery.*

In ninth grade a boy named Tim had died suddenly, over a weekend. The cause was something called an aneurysm. Blood leaking through the brain and swelling the skull.

Easy. Fast.

But, no: Matt wasn't going to be morbid. Ursula Riggs

was his friend, and was helping him. And Mr Weinberg. And others were helping him. He knew.

"Suburban hysteria" – the *Times* reporter was the only journalist so far to be shrewd enough to perceive what was happening. Still, the small, single-paragraph piece had run on the front page of the Metro Section where everyone in Rocky River who read *The New York Times*, which was more or less everybody in Rocky River, would see it.

Stacey Flynn hadn't e-mailed or called Matt, either. Or any of the four or five girls with whom he'd have said he was "good friends". By Monday morning he'd stopped expecting to hear from them, and he'd stopped (he told himself) feeling bad about it.

They had their reasons, Matt supposed.

Then, finally. Late Sunday night. Three of the guys e-mailed Matt. (A conspiracy?)

Hi Matt--
This really sucks, its so stupid.

But my dad (who is going to vet this [hi Dad!] not
that we have censorship in this Democrat-registered
household) says I'd better "keep clear" of the mess for a
while. Our lawyer "advises". So I can't answer your e-mails
etc right now.

Talk to you another time, OK?
neil

HI MATT
I TOLD THEM EVERYTHING. THAT IT WAS A JOKE. I THINK
THEY BELIEVE ME. (I'M NOT SURE.) BUT I CANT
"COMMUNICATE" WITH YOU RIGHT NOW. SORRY MATT.
HOPE YOU UNDERSTAND.

SKEET

Hi Matt,
Sorry not to get back to you. I feel bad about this. But things
will be OK soon. Can't write much now. All e-mail exists in
cyberspace, you know. It's eternal.

The police are OK. Just trying to get to the bottom of this.

Russ

Matt reread these messages a dozen times. Like those
knotty little poems of Emily Dickinson in their American lit
anthology. There was meaning hidden inside the words, and
between the words. It didn't require a rocket scientist to
decipher much of it.

Matt e-mailed Mr Weinberg:

Monday/Quarantine/Solitary Confinement

Mr Weinberg,
I guess I'm a leper there? Nobody can "communicate" with me?
Like it would be considered a "conspiracy"?
WHAT ARE PEOPLE SAYING?

Matt "Terrorist" Donaghy

Matt hesitated before pressing SEND. Maybe this wasn't a good idea? Sure, the cops were reading e-mail. Any e-mail from Matt Donaghy they'd read. If it weren't for Mr Leacock, they'd have confiscated Matt's computer. And maybe, if the investigation continued, they would.

Anyway, Matt sent his message to Mr Weinberg. And Mr Weinberg didn't reply.

Matt overheard his dad talking earnestly, angrily on the phone.

With Mr Leacock, he guessed.

". . . sue *them*! That's what we'll do! Parrish, and the school district, and... the 'witnesses'. And whoever else is responsible! They can't do this to my son, and to the Donaghys...."

*Yeah? They can't?*

Hiking in the nature preserve. In his boots, on the icy boulders of Rocky River Creek. Pumpkin panted along behind him, whimpering at times because she couldn't keep up. Snow and ice encrusted her big clumsy paws. Her tail thumping halfheartedly. The sky overhead was still tarnished like something badly scoured. But Matt's heart was beating hard, and he was feeling good. What had Ursula Riggs written – FINGERS CROSSED FOR JUSTICE.

*She* believed Matt, for sure. She must like him, too. Even if nobody else did.

Matt heard it all, in his mom's excited voice.

"Matt! Good news! Pick up the phone."

He hadn't had time even to blow his nose. He picked up the phone receiver, and his hand was trembling.

And it was Mr Leacock with the news Matt had been hoping for all weekend – "Matt? It's settled. You're no longer suspended. They're going to call it, officially, a 'misunderstanding'. They're going to issue an apology. Be back in school tomorrow, like nothing was ever wrong."

Matt was grinning as if he'd won the lottery.

Before supper that night he e-mailed Ursula Riggs with his good news:

Dear Ursula--
Its OFFICIAL. Matt Donaghy is NOT A TERRORIST. THANK YOU THANK YOU THANK YOU.
                              Your friend Matt

# February

# tEN

"Hi, ursula!"

I used to be shy at school but Ugly Girl was never shy.

I used to walk with my eyes lowered, hoping nobody would see me if I didn't see them, but Ugly Girl never lowered her eyes.

I used to hope nobody would bump into me, but now other people keep clear of Ugly Girl, not wanting Ugly Girl to bump into them. Ugly Girl striding through the universe!

But now even Ugly Girl, whenever she saw Matt Donaghy, wanted to shrink away in shyness.

"Hi, Ursula..."

The voice came out of the air. It was a friendly-hopeful voice.

"Ursula? Hi. You coming this way... ?"

Matt Donaghy called out, smiling. Since he'd been suspended from school, then "reinstated", Matt smiled a lot.

This morning he was waiting on the stairs going up to homeroom; kids were passing him going up, and I was headed in that direction too. Obviously I was headed in that direction, where else? Matt and I were both in Mrs Carlisle's homeroom.

"Ursula...?"

A weird hot flash came over me; my face burned. It was like, in the game with Tarrytown, I knew I was going to be tripped, a fraction of a second before I fell. I thought, *I'm going to trip on the stairs.*

It was because Matt Donaghy was there, watching me.

Matt Donaghy, smiling at me.

Matt Donaghy. Who signed his e-mail *Your friend Matt.*

My face shut up like a fist. My eyes went steely and I smiled a forced little half smile like I'd have smiled at Mr Parrish, just to be polite. *Ugly Girl is polite!*

Without knowing what I was doing exactly, I turned away from the stairs and walked blindly in another direction. Into the senior wing where everybody was opening lockers, talking, and laughing with one another. And Ugly Girl in their midst, tall and fast striding in her satin school jacket, Mets cap, and khakis and boots. *What's she doing here? Wow. Big Ursula Riggs.*

I saw, but did not acknowledge, the faces of Trevor Cassity and his jock buddies. I saw, but did not acknowledge, the startled-and-then-expressionless face of Courtney Levao, one of the girls on the basketball team.

If there was talk around school that I'd quit the team cold, I ignored it.

If there was talk that my teammates and Ms Schultz were glad to be rid of Ugly Girl, I ignored it.

Ugly Girl, warrior-woman. Going her own way.

I took another stairway up to homeroom. The bell was ringing when I came in and took my seat. Dumped my backpack on the floor. If Matt Donaghy was in his seat (third row to the left from mine, two desks back) talking and laughing with his buddies, Ugly Girl wasn't going to notice.

# E/EVEN

Dear Ursula--
I'm wondering, is something wrong? Around school, you aren't
very friendly. (Of course, nobody is, much. Except to my face
when they have to be.) I guess you must've got my e-mail
THANKING YOU? I sent it right away. As soon as I heard.

I said THANK YOU THANK YOU THANK YOU.

It's been 14 days now. Since I was "taken into custody" etc. No,
I'm not counting (consciously). Like I died, & was brought back to
life. Except it's "life"--not like it used to be. I can't explain.

I'm wondering maybe my messages are not getting to you?
I sent three.

I shouldn't complain I suppose, it's over now. The newspapers & TV are on to other things. Anything local, it's got to be exaggerated I guess. Nothing much happens in Rocky River except people live & die, & some of them betray their best friends.

Mr Weinberg says try to forget & forgive. Sure!

(You aren't mad at me, Ursula, are you? Or maybe--your parents are telling you not to "communicate" with me any more?)

What subject are you going to write on, for History? I thought I would write of how so many Northerners hated Lincoln & drew caricatures of him as an ape / "Negro"-ape. & how his enemies celebrated when he was assassinated. While Abraham Lincoln is considered such a hero to us today, he was hated & reviled in his own time. & that time was when he lived.

February sucks! Even the snow is ugly & pocked. Every day is a Nothing Day. I skipped class meeting, couldn't face it. (You probably skipped, too. But I'm the VP.)

My word for this is NOTHING-TIME. Like, today is a NOTHING-DAY. This is a NOTHING-HOUR. Everything tastes like burned toast & smells like gym socks.

Your friend Matt-the-Mouth

89

Matt hesitated a long time with this. If he pressed SEND, it was gone to Ursula Riggs in a heartbeat. And couldn't be retrieved, or erased.

*All e-mail exists in cyberspace. It's eternal.*

(Who'd said that? Matt's old friend from grade school, Russ Mercer. Except they weren't friends, much, any longer. Hard to say why.)

Instead of pressing SEND, Matt pressed DELETE.

Easier that way.

# tWElvE

*Ugly Girl, principal's pet!*

This really weird bizarre thing.

My homeroom teacher, Mrs Carlisle, told me please to drop by Mr Parrish's office before going to my next class, and I told her I'd be late for biology if I went all the way downstairs to the front office, and Mrs Carlisle said not to worry, I'd be given a pink slip.

So, wondering what old Parrish wanted, I went to see him.

Was Ugly Girl in some trouble I didn't know about? I behaved myself in Schultz's gym classes and uttered not a sarcastic word except, sometimes, under my breath. I practised baskets by myself when the gym was open and nobody much was around. Had Schultz complained about me to Parrish? Was it against the law to quit a school team?

But – what a surprise! Mr Parrish was on his feet and came to shake my hand.

He was embarrassed, but you could see he was sincere.

What a weird old guy.

Telling me in this voice like a speech at assembly that I'd behaved "very maturely" and "responsibly" in recent weeks. During the "crisis". He apologised he hadn't had time to tell me in person, but he wanted me to know.

"Sure, Mr Parrish. OK."

"We're putting it all behind us, now. It was a misunderstanding pure and simple."

"Yeah. I guess."

"Mrs Hale and I have written up a very positive report on your participation, Ursula. You behaved like a true citizen of our little commonwealth here at Rocky River High." Mr Parrish paused. "College admissions officers will be impressed, I think, with what we've written about you. I mean, sometime in the future. I'm also drafting a letter to your parents. Commending them on their daughter's exemplary behaviour at a time when others were behaving..."

Hysterically. Right!

Mr Parrish brooded, pushing his glasses against the bridge of his pudgy nose. "Of course, we did have to be... cautious."

"Sure, Mr Parrish."

The principal continued, a little less certainly, "Is it your general sense, Ursula, that the crisis has been more or less forgotten?"

I nodded, sure. I guessed so.

"No one is talking about it... any more?"

I shrugged. I guessed not.

"Do you... talk to Matt Donaghy, ever?"

"No."

"You don't! Ever... ?"

"No."

*I am not a friend of Matt Donaghy's. I defended him purely on principle.*

During the "crisis" as Mr Parrish called it, Rocky River High had drawn more publicity than ever before in its history. Not the kind of publicity anybody wants, though.

Generally it was believed that Mr Parrish and his staff had dealt with the crisis intelligently, and the school board had issued a formal statement backing them. Matt Donaghy's name had never been released to the media. But sure, everyone knew.

Still, I didn't believe they were talking about it any more. It had become Boring. There were other subjects on people's minds.

Mr Parrish was smiling in that strained hopeful way adults have when they want you to think something they aren't a hundred per cent certain of themselves. So if you go away thinking it, they can think it, too. Or maybe.

"Again, Ursula – thank you. You can pick up a pink slip from my secretary to explain being late for class."

Was I supposed to thank *him*? I didn't.


On the stairs going down to the cafeteria I heard a rude loud whistle, shrill as a referee's whistle. "Hey Ursula! Are you mad at me, or what?"

It was Bonnie LeMoyne. Skinny wiry funny unpredictable Bonnie I'd been avoiding since the Tarrytown game. Bonnie who (I'd sort of thought) was mad at *me*.

"No. Why'd I be?"

Bonnie snorted with laughter. "Oh, sure. You look right through me, Urs. Like, I'm sitting in the cafeteria waving at you, and you don't see me. Right?"

Ugly Girl had to laugh, Bonnie had a way of being funny about dopey behaviour. You could see how you appeared to her, and why it was funny, but your pride wasn't injured, somehow.

She'd called me Urs. This was Bonnie's name for me since grade school and she pronounced it in a hissing growl: *Errrrrssss!* Hearing it, I felt a warmth in my heart for Bonnie LeMoyne. We weren't going to talk about the team, I vowed.

I knew that Rocky River hadn't been doing too well since I'd quit. I didn't know if I was happy that they were losing without me or kind of sad. Mostly, I tried not to think about it.

Ugly Girl was skilled at that. Cutting off things she didn't want to think about.

We had lunch. It was like old times. Or almost. Eveann McDowd came by. Since Eveann helped me out talking to Mr Parrish, she was Ugly Girl's best friend. I really liked Eveann now. I even liked her cranky mom.

We were talking, and laughing pretty loud, and I saw Matt Donaghy coming through the cafeteria line. My mind just went blank.

I couldn't even see if he was alone, or with his friends.

I swallowed, hard. It was so weird, as if the breath just went out of me.

Like on the basketball court, when somebody'd jabbed her elbow right into my chest. Knocked the air out of my lungs.

What was happening to Ugly Girl? It was scary, almost.

Bonnie was telling us some comical story, and at the same time I was panicked thinking: what if Matt sees me, what if he comes over to say hi, what if he asks to sit with us... I hoped he'd given up trying to be friends with me. He'd sent two or three e-mail messages and he'd even called and left messages on my voice mail but I never called back. I hated the phone. Even calling friends, Ugly Girl was uncomfortable.

"Ursula? What's wrong?"

"What? Nothing."

I scowled, so Bonnie and Eveann would drop the subject.

Matt hadn't seen me. He carried his tray to the far side of the cafeteria. To sit with his friends, I guess. That circle. Preppies and preppie-jocks. I never looked, I had no curiosity.

Near the end of lunch hour Bonnie leaned across the table and said, "It's pretty pathetic without you on the team, Urs. Sleepy Hollow walked all over us last week, you heard? Schultz was practically in tears."

Sure. I'd heard. It would've been hard to miss the headline in our school paper. SLEEPY HOLLOW TROUNCES RR 36–22, GIRLS' BASKETBALL.

I leaned across the table too. "You want the rest of that yogurt, Bonnie? If not—"

It was the sappy sugary fruit yogurt, not my favourite. But Ugly Girl was hungry.

# thirtEEN

It Was a Friday afternoon in February, after classes. Two weeks and one day after Matt Donaghy's "arrest".

Another Nothing-Day. Smelling of dirty socks, and worse.

Matt had made his decision. Nothing would deflect him from his decision. Though Mr Bernhardt winced, just visibly. "Matt, I'm sure this isn't necessary."

But the junior class advisor spoke so slowly, with such embarrassment, Matt picked up the opposite message.

*Not necessary, but a good idea.*

Matt was resigning his vice presidency of the junior class. This elected office he'd been so ridiculously, pathetically proud of.

"No one's said anything to you, Matt, have they?"

"No."

Matt laughed. *No one's said anything to me, much. That's just it.*

"Then why resign?"

"I only won by eleven votes, Mr Bernhardt. If the election was now, I'd lose."

Mr Bernhardt was looking at Matt Donaghy quizzically. (Pityingly?) Matt was taking Intro to German from this teacher, and his grades had been A–/B+ in the fall semester and had plummeted to C/C– in recent weeks. *Nicht sehr gut.* No, not very good. But German wasn't the subject of this brief conference.

Maybe Mr Bernhardt was surprised that a sixteen-year-old "average" student would reason so logically? For it was true, of course. Except Matt Donaghy wouldn't even be nominated to run for class office now.

Mr Bernhardt began to speak, then fell silent. Outside the second-floor window, voices lifted from the walk below. Muffled voices, laughter. Matt felt lighthearted suddenly. "So. I'm formally resigned, I guess?"

"Better put it in writing, Matt," Mr Bernhardt said. You could see he was both embarrassed and relieved. "Just for the record."

# fourteen

It Was a Monday afternoon in February, after classes. Two weeks, four days after Matt Donaghy's "arrest".

Another Nothing-Day. Smelling of dirty socks, and worse.

"Matt, we just can't."

"Can't – what?"

"We can't print this in the paper."

"Why not, Mr Steiner?"

"It's too... accusing. And it isn't very funny."

Matt felt his lower jaw tighten. He'd been gritting, grinding his teeth lately. During the night, in his troubled sleep. But now he smiled. Tried to smile. Was it an ugly, angry smile? He was trying for the nice-guy preppie smile he'd always worn.

He hadn't realised he was trembling. He clenched his fists, dug his nails into the palms of his hands.

He saw Mr Steiner glance at his fists. Just a quick startled glance.

"You mean, like, if it was 'funnier' it would be OK?"

"I didn't say that, exactly."

"Why isn't it funny, Mr Steiner? Isn't the truth 'funny'?"

Matt's column was meant to be humorous. "Just for the Record..."

A comical letter of resignation written by an individual you realise, gradually, is "resigning" from life: he's about to be given a lethal injection for the crime of being mistaken for a "famous and glamorous serial killer". But the medical technician who administers the injection can't find a usable vein. Until finally, the needle has to be inserted into the condemned man's eye...

"Sometimes the truth is funny, or can be made funny," Mr Steiner said slowly, "but sometimes... humour can fall flat, it's just too raw."

"It isn't too long, is it?"

"Matt, it just isn't *funny*."

"Is everything in the paper funny? Every article, every photo? I never noticed that."

"Matt, don't get excited. This is—"

"Mr Steiner, I'm not excited. I'm just, like, puzzled. Am I being censored by just you, or by the whole staff?"

There was a pained silence. Mr Steiner, faculty advisor of the school paper, the youngest teacher at Rocky River and one of the most popular, was frowning at Matt. Whom he'd always liked. Whose "wild sense of humour" he'd praised. Now he was holding a copy of Matt's "Just for the Record" between his fingers as you might hold something that gave off a distinct odour.

"The editors did confer with me, yes. That's why I'm talking with you about the piece. They thought—"

"So you're all censoring me, then?"

His friends. The editor, the features editor. The twelve-member staff. They must've had a secret meeting. To discuss Matt Donaghy. Behind his back.

Mr Steiner winced. The word "censor" was a politically incorrect word. You could see it hurt this man, almost physically, to be so accused.

"'Censoring' is – is not – what this is about, Matt. It's a matter of – good taste. Under the circumstances."

"What circumstances? That I'm a formerly accused 'psychoterrorist' who ought to be grateful he isn't in prison? That I should be extra grateful I'm allowed back to school at all?"

Matt's heart was beating hard. He couldn't believe that his mouth was uttering such words. He liked this! He liked the truth being exposed at last instead of disguised behind vague mumbles, averted eyes. And he liked Mr Steiner on his feet, facing Matt. He liked seeing that Mr Steiner, a math teacher revered for being quite a jock, a serious marathon runner, five feet nine to Matt's five feet eleven, was getting visibly nervous.

"Matt, maybe you should make an appointment – to talk to Mr Rainey?"

Matt shook his head, sneering. Rainey! The school shrink.

"I can understand your bitterness, Matt, and confusion—"

"I'm not confused, Mr Steiner. *I'm* not."

"It was a painful episode. Everyone regrets it. But it's over now, and the best remedy for healing is—"

"'Forgive and forget.' Or is it – 'forget and forgive'?"

Matt laughed so harshly, Mr Steiner stared at him.

This strange, angry edge to Matt Donaghy! His smile had grown ironic, suspicious. He looked taller, leaner, like a knife blade. Even his freckles looked bleached out. His faded-red hair was longer; he had a habit of brushing it impatiently out of his eyes. His skin looked roughened, as if he'd been rubbing it with sandpaper. He'd overheard his mother saying to his father, *"He isn't a boy any longer. He's changed."*

Matt hoped this was true. He'd had enough of being a good American *boy*.

When he'd returned to school after the suspension, he'd been like a small kid at Christmas. So excited and hopeful. He'd expected – what? Something like a welcoming committee? Handshakes, hugs and kisses? And apologies? Stacey Flynn, tears in her eyes, kissing his cheek and saying, "Oh, Matt. We're all so sorry. We never doubted you, Matt. *We love you.*"

He hadn't even seen Stacey, that first morning.

Maybe he'd been unrealistic? He'd expected too much? Opening his locker that morning in the noisy junior corridor, glancing around with a self-conscious smile, waiting for people to notice him... Sure, Skeet and Neil and Cal and Russ and others were friendly enough. Friendly seeming. Kids whose lockers were next to Matt's, and who sat next to him in classes. But they were embarrassed too. They didn't know what to say. Russ, who never lacked for words, was stammering, "That was really weird, I guess.... It must've been... weird." Even Mr Weinberg, cloaking his unease in witticisms, wasn't the same with Matt. And when Matt did encounter Stacey, after classes, she was rushing to choir rehearsal and said, flush-faced, "Oh, Matt! I'll call you – soon!"

Of course, Stacey never called.

It was like Matt had been wounded somewhere on his body he couldn't see, and the wound was visible to others, raw and ugly. When they looked at him, they saw just the wound. They weren't seeing *Matt Donaghy* any longer.

Even Ursula Riggs, who'd testified on his behalf, avoided him. Why?

Matt had written "Just for the Record" to express how it felt, but to be funny about it, too. Now Mr Steiner and the staff of the newspaper, who he'd believed were his friends, were telling him it wasn't funny. It wasn't in "good taste".

Life was a big balloon slowly leaking air, deflating.

"Matt? You can understand our perspective, can't you?"

Mr Steiner was looking "sincerely" at Matt in that way that all the teachers were doing lately. They were being "earnest" – maybe they thought they were being "profound". Sure, he knew that most of them, who knew him, had defended him. But that wasn't enough.

Mr Steiner had been one of Matt's friends, he'd thought. But now Matt could see that Steiner wasn't his friend either.

Matt took the copy of "Just for the Record" back from the teacher and tore it into long strips. Steiner winced, saying, "Matt, c'mon. Don't be childish. You're taking this too seriously. As an editor, you've turned people down."

"Sure. People who can't write. People with nothing to say and no idea how to say it."

"This isn't your best writing, Matt. In a few weeks—"

"That's what the paper publishes, 'best writing'? Like, everybody in the *Rocky River Run* is a Pulitzer Prize winner?"

"—in a few weeks you'll be grateful we didn't print it. Believe me, Matt."

"Sure. Thanks, Mr Steiner."

Matt's voice was so laced with sarcasm, it tasted like poison in his mouth.

Steiner, trying to be upbeat, walked with Matt to the door of his office. If the teacher laid a hand on Matt's shoulder, big-brother crap, Matt was going to shrug it off.

But Steiner didn't.

Dear Mr Steiner:
This is "just for the record..." I am resigning from the "Rocky River Run" staff.
                              The Rocky River Psychoterrorist

Matt laughed, typing up this message. But no, better not send it. Big Mouth had gotten into enough trouble this term.

Dear Mr Steiner:
It is with regret but necessity that I am resigning from the "Rocky River Run" staff.
                              Matthew Donaghy

Matt clicked SEND. And presto – it was gone.

"This is getting easier and easier, Pumpkin. I'm liking the feeling."

Pumpkin, misinterpreting Matt's mood for happiness, thumped her tail and nudged her eager head against him to be petted.

"Hey, Matt? Is something wrong?"

"'Something wrong'? With who?"

Matt saw Alex wince. He said, relenting, "I got work to do. Math, it's a bummer."

Matt eased the door shut on Alex.

When you feel such total disgust with the world, it's best not to infect other, innocent people.

*One thing you don't want to do, Big Mouth. Bring Alex down to your level of existence.*

Gordon Kim will assume the vice presidency of the junior class, as Matt Donaghy has resigned. Gordon was runner-up in last fall's election.

This terse item appeared in the school paper, the *Rocky River Run*, on the Friday following Matt's resignation. It was buried on page four, without a headline.

Seeing it, Matt laughed aloud.

What had he been expecting, a front-page photo spread?

Now people had another reason to stare at Matt when they thought he wasn't seeing them, and to look quickly away when it became evident he was. In Tower Records at the mall, Matt ran into three girls from the junior class, and one of them, Wendy Diehl, who was in Matt's history class, said, with a curious downturning of her lips, "Hi, Matt Donaghy. *I* voted for you." The three girls giggled, and Matt blushed, and stammered, "Thanks," and walked away.

What did this mean? That they supported him?

The president of the junior class, who'd campaigned hard for the office, was a high-energy, political-minded girl named Sandra Friedman who already spoke of hoping to get accepted by Harvard Law in five years' time. She told Matt she was sorry to hear he'd resigned, but – "It's kind of a nothing job, vice president, I guess," Sandra said tactlessly. "It's not like you have anything to *do.*"

The only other person to speak to Matt about his resignation was the kid who'd replaced him, Gordon Kim, a popular Korean-American transfer from Berkeley. He'd entered the election as a joke. Gordon, a math genius, behaved as if he thought most Rocky River events were jokes; he hadn't seemed to catch on to why Matt was resigning. "Any time you want to be vice president again, it's OK with me, Matt. *You* won the election."

None of Matt's friends, who'd helped him campaign, spoke of his resignation. To his face, anyway.

*My heart is a stone.*
*I can feel it hardening.*

Leaving the school library, Friday afternoon. God damn! He had to pass by some of his friends, hanging out by the stairs. They were talking about a party that weekend. Russ Mercer saw Matt, and blushed, and caught up with him on the stairs. "Hey, Matt? How's it going?" and Matt shrugged, not looking at Russ, who'd been one of his closest friends since sixth grade, and Russ said, guiltily, "We're just making plans to get together... want to join us?" and Matt said with a stiff, fixed smile, "Thanks, but I'm busy all weekend. Thanks, Russ."

> *Thanks, Russ.*
> *Thanks to all of you.*
> *My heart is a stone – it won't be broken again.*

Matt Donaghy loved his mom and dad. He did! But now he was starting to hate them. These are the things they said to him, to his face.

> **Things are fine, Matt!**
> **It won't be on your school record, Mr Parrish promised!**
> **Try to put it behind you, Matt.**
> **Don't be moping!**
> ***Please* let Evita get into your room to clean it, will you?**
> **You'll feel better when...**
> **It's just the weather...**
> **In a few weeks...**

And when they believed Matt wasn't listening, these are the things they said in lowered, anxious voices.

> **I can't talk to him any longer.**
> **He won't talk to *me*.**

He isn't himself. He's changed.

He's sarcastic, he's hostile.

His room *smells*.

He's depressed. I know what depression is.

I'm exhausted too.

I can't sleep and I'm exhausted.

He's rude to Alex. Alex loves him.

I hate this community. I used to love it.

I know what depression is, and Mr Parrish and the
school district are to blame.

He refuses to let me make an appointment for him
to see a...

He refuses to let Evita into his room to clean it,
and his room *smells*.

I know what depression is, and it's blanketing this
house like smog.

Matt Donaghy loved his mom and dad. But now he was
starting to hate them.

# fifteen

Dear Ursula,

I saw you in school yesterday. *Not* seeing me. Or if
you did, you looked right through me. (Maybe I'm a ghost?)

OK--I understand. (I guess.) Big Mouth Donaghy isn't cool &
Ursula Riggs is one of Rocky River's coolest individuals.

(I'm not going to harass you like some nut, I promise. This is
the final time I will write.)

(It's just... I'm so lonely.)

I think people wanted me--or somebody--to be the
psychoterrorist. When it didn't turn out, they were-
-are--disappointed.

Ursula, who were the "witnesses" who reported me? Do you know? I keep asking myself: did they hate me so much? Did they really really HATE ME SO MUCH? Or--did they think they were reporting the truth?

Ursula Riggs is cool because: 1) You don't give a damn for them. Their false eyes & smiling mask faces. 2) You are YOU. Everybody respects that.

I never used to be lonely at home, but now I hate them talking to me. They act like I'm sick. They want me to see a shrink. (Sure! "For the record.") Maybe I can get a prescription for Prozac, like Mom. She says it "helps her cope".

My dad is away a lot, & when he's home he is tired & distracted. He blames me (I know) for jeopardising his job. His company is superconscious of "image". I have sullied the name DONAGHY. I know that Dad & Mom are ashamed of me though they're careful not to say so to my face.

It's true. Except for Big Mouth none of this trouble would have happened.

My heart is a stone, & I like the feeling. I guess.

They think I'm "depressed". I'm not, I am only seeing now the TRUTH.

I wish you could be my friend, Ursula. The girls I used to know,

I don't trust now. You're different--you're not a "girl"--like them.

Even your name--URSULA. It's special.

(OK, I'm through. I promise I won't write again.)
                              Your friend Matt Donaghy

It was two forty-seven A.M. Matt was hunched over his
computer, sweaty and anxious. He hadn't been able to
concentrate on his schoolwork, which seemed so trivial now,
and he'd avoided eating dinner with his mom and Alex, and
he'd wasted hours clicking around on the Internet looking for
people worse off than himself, and now this crazy dorky letter
to Ursula Riggs – this was the weirdest behaviour yet.

He could imagine Skeet's reaction if Skeet knew.

*Matt's got a crush on Big Ursula?*

He could imagine Stacey's reaction...

But nobody really knew Ursula Riggs. She stood outside all
the cliques. She truly was special.

She was the only one who'd defended him.

*Not enough that Matt's got himself into trouble, now he's
hanging out with Ursula Riggs. Weird!*

*Big Mouth's desperate, that's the reason.*

Matt reread his e-mail to Ursula and decided not to click
SEND, but DELETE.

Are you sure? Y/N.

Y. Matt was sure.

If the guys had known, they'd have approved.

# sixtEEN

**Ugly Girl, Warrior-Woman.**

*Ugly Girl, flying high in Manhattan.*

That wasn't the plan, for sure. Poor Mom!

How this adventure began was, Mom goes: "Ursula, we hardly ever see you any more. Lisa misses you." When I don't say anything, but am feeling a little guilty, Mom adds, "Lisa looks up to you, honey. You're her big sister." (Like I'm Frankenstein, or something. B I G.) "I'll get tickets for the three of us, this isn't ballet but modern dance and I think you'll like it. We can have lunch at Fiorello's before the matinee, come on, honey, say *yes.*"

You'd have to see this scene to believe it. Why Ugly Girl gave in, with a shrug. OK, Mom. Mom was actually stroking my hair that needed washing, and sort of tickling the nape of my neck like I was a big cat, and I liked the feeling, I guess. I liked Mom OK, sometimes. She was so proud of me when Mr

Parrish sent his letter, even more than Dad. She'd admitted it was wrong – "cowardly" – of her to beg me not to get involved, she was "very sorry" she'd tried to interfere. Dad wasn't so sure, I guess.

So anyway, I said OK. And Mom bought three tickets for this Sunday matinee at Lincoln Centre. And there was the joke in our household then that Ursula agreed to come into the city with Mom and Lisa to see a dance programme mainly because of having lunch at Fiorello's before the matinee. Dad said, "There's a gal after my own stomach."

Since quitting the team I'd been running more, and hiking, in the Rocky River Nature Preserve. I shot baskets in the gym if nobody was around. At home I lifted twenty-pound dumbbells, Dad's weights he hadn't touched in years, to firm up my arm and shoulder muscles so they wouldn't get flaccid. Actually I guessed my weight was down by a few pounds, because my clothes didn't fit tight like they sometimes did. Ugly Girl never weighed herself. I knew there were girls at school, and my own kid sister and Mom, who weighed themselves every morning like fanatics. I only found out what I weighed when I had to get examined by a doctor or nurse. Who cares what you weigh? It's a Very Boring Fact.

When I was a young girl, beginning at age nine, what I'd loved best was swimming. Swimming and diving. Diving and swimming! Our coach for the team in middle school used to say to us, "Happy flying, girls!" If it was an outdoor pool, you'd be flying into the sky. And slicing into the water like a knife blade, so clean. But I was growing fast. Most of the other girls stayed skinny except for me. My thighs, hips and breasts were taking shape as if every night while I slept a sculptor was adding flesh to me, like clay.

One day, when I was in eighth grade, I heard my dad say to my mom, "She's getting big, isn't she?" They were in another room; I wasn't supposed to hear.

Another time Dad said to me, "Ursula, you're getting to be a big girl." It was like he had more to say, but stopped. His eyes were on my face, like he didn't want to look anywhere else.

The next swim practice, I looked at myself in a mirror in the locker room and I saw this fattish, chunky girl. Not like the other girls. I could hardly make myself leave the locker room and go out to the pool. *Thunder thighs* was something the older boys said to girls; I'd overheard it without understanding what they meant, exactly. But now I knew.

At the next meet I froze on the diving board, my knees were shaking so. I ran back into the locker room trying not to cry, but that was the end of the swim team for me. Luckily, other sports like soccer, field hockey, basketball had uniforms that could be pretty loose. You could almost hide inside them.

This time in February, when Mom took us to New York to see the dance troupe, was a weird sort of secretive time for me. I never told Mom and Dad exactly why I'd quit the team when it had meant so much to me. Maybe I didn't know exactly why. I never told them about how disgusted I felt towards most of the kids at school, for the way they'd behaved over Matt Donaghy and the "bomb scare". Like they'd wanted to believe it was true. Like it was the most excitement they'd had in a long time. For sure, I never told them how guilty I felt for acting like everybody else, turning away from Matt when he came back to school.

Lately, I hated being touched. Just accidental touching, brushing against. It reminded me of being tripped on the basketball court, elbowed in the chest, and crowded by the Tarrytown team like a pack of hyenas moving in for the kill.

Like the outermost layer of my skin had been peeled away, and anything that touched me, however lightly, could hurt.

There were kids who liked to bump into people at school like it was an "accident". There'd always been kids like this, mostly guys, starting in grade school. Like sex perverts. For sure, no guy would dare to brush against Ugly Girl for such a reason! Sometimes it was done to hurt, or to provoke. Sometimes – who knows why? Like the Brewer twins, Muriel and Miriam, who were seniors, mean smirky girls nobody liked or trusted. They wore navy-blue skirts and baggy shirts and jackets like uniforms. Their father was a controversial local character, Reverend "Ike" Brewer, who had his own small church, Apostles of Jesus, where he preached against sex education in public schools, public funds for AIDS research, affirmative action, and "giving a free ride" to feminists, gays, blacks, "ethnic minorities". In middle school Brewer petitioned to get a long list of books banned from our library (including *Black Beauty*, which he seemed to think was a Black Muslim novel). Last year at Rocky River he'd led a nasty campaign to get one of our new young teachers, Mr Steiner, fired because Mr Steiner had marched in the gay pride parade in Manhattan and "wasn't to be entrusted" with young people. (Both campaigns failed. But caused a lot of upset and hard feelings, and drew a disgusting amount of media attention.) The Brewer twins were girls with faces like sour puddings. They were C-minus students with no sports or activities because their parents disapproved of them "mixing" with the rest of us. Every morning Reverend Brewer dropped Muriel and Miriam off at school, and every afternoon he picked them up, in a worn-looking minivan with a JESUS SAVES sticker on the front bumper and on the rear WELCOME TO AMERICA, NOW EITHER SPEAK ENGLISH OR LEAVE IT.

I guess "religious" people like Reverend Brewer don't have a clue what America means.

One February morning the Brewer twins were headed upstairs with me, and sort of pushing and crowding against me, and when I turned I saw the two of them flush faced and smirking. "Hey! What're you doing?" I asked. I clenched my fists like I was going to attack them, and one of them said breathlessly, "You wouldn't dare, you big horse! You'd be arrested for assault." The other said, "You'd be *sued*. We know who you are." Which was Muriel Brewer, and which was Miriam? Nobody could tell. Each had dark hair parted on the left side of her head, and each had a squeaky, nasal voice. "You wouldn't dare hurt us, you big bully. Think you're so important!" The other said, turning her lower lip downward and inside out, tempting me to punch her, "S'pose you're real proud of yourself, huh? Sticking up for somebody wants to blow up the school. Sucking up to the prin-ci-pal. Jew-girl!"

People were staring at us, edging quickly away out of fear there'd be a fight. The Brewer twins were at least three inches shorter than me, and they were no kind of athletes, not at all. Ugly Girl could've lifted them and tossed them down the stairs headfirst.

Don't think I wasn't contemplating doing just that.

My heart was pounding like crazy. "Get away from me! Go to hell," I said.

Muriel and Miriam ran down the stairs giggling. One screamed back over her shoulder, "*You're* the one who's gonna go to hell, Jew-girl!"

For sure I didn't tell Mom and Dad about the crazy Brewer twins.

Dad was always saying that people like Reverend Brewer were very dangerous in our society. The United States was a multicultural society, but there was still a lot of prejudice against ethnic minorities. Obviously. There was still a lot of anti-Semitism, though it was mostly hidden. Reverend Brewer was like a man striking a match in a dried-out forest. He knew exactly what he was doing. But he could always say he was preaching "God's word".

It was all so weird. I wasn't even Jewish!

In the Brewers' mean mouths, the term "Jew-girl" sounded like an obscenity. I guess that's how they meant it. Something they'd been hearing at home.

What I really wondered was why they'd taunted me – "Sticking up for somebody wants to blow up the school." How'd they know?

Evidently it had become common knowledge that I'd talked to Mr Parrish. Maybe Matt Donaghy had told his friends.

Actually, I wasn't that proud of myself. Whenever I'm singled out for attention, even praise, I get really self-conscious.

Big deal. Harold Parrish, principal, had sent a letter to Mr and Mrs Clayton Riggs commending them on their daughter's "good citizenship". Sure, it was a form letter the shrewd old guy had sent to dozens of important people in the school district, changing names and details, of course. I was sort of ashamed when my parents showed me the letter, as if I'd gone to see Mr Parrish just to impress him.

*Please understand that as principal of Rocky River High School I had to weigh the safety and rights of the majority... against the rights of the individual. At no time did I, or my colleagues, seriously believe the allegations made against Matthew Donaghy, who is one of the school's outstanding students. In the light of school violence across the nation in recent years, and parental anxiety about the safety of their children, I believed that the necessary thing to do was behave with extreme caution.*

Sure: calling in the cops. Practically calling in the reporters and TV crews.

*For any inconveniences caused, and emotional distress, my staff and I are truly sorry. But through the responsible citizenship of your daughter Ursula, as well as the thoroughness of our investigation, this difficult episode came to a satisfactory ending.*

Tell that to Matt Donaghy.

My dad made a photocopy of the letter to give to me "for my files". As soon as I was alone I tore it into pieces.

I was thinking of Mr Parrish's phony letter, and the nasty Brewer twins, and Matt Donaghy, when Mom, Lisa and I took our seats in the plushy theatre at Lincoln Centre. What a fancy, fussy place! Chandeliers, and the mostly older-female audience murmuring in a kind of churchy hush. I was wearing my satin Rocky River jacket, and my khakis, and the faux palomino boots that were kind of beat up by the winter and funky looking. Mom made me take off the Mets cap. I'd stuffed it in my pocket. For dress-up I'd put in all my ear studs – nine in each ear. (Not that they matched.) I felt big and clumsy as a horse trapped in a tinsel candy box. Even in the restaurant I was distracted and sort of sullen. Thinking how people like the Brewers could poison the world for you with their meanness. Ugly Girl was tough but never mean – I hoped. Mom chided me for my "bull-dog face" but I didn't laugh. Lisa was chattering about the dance troupe; she just picked at the food on her plate. Luscious spinach linguine heaped with specialty mushrooms. Lisa was always picking at her food lately, I'd been noticing. Even my brown rice/tofu casserole with broccoli and nuts that she used to love. The waiter would have taken Lisa's plate away except I stopped him. "*I'll* eat that." Mom was embarrassed – that wasn't the way a well-mannered young lady from the upscale suburb Rocky River behaved.

Right. It wasn't.

Five minutes into a dance called *Sylvan Sunset* I knew I had to escape from this place or I'd suffocate. My knees kept hitting against the seat in front of me, and the woman sitting there would glance around to glare – I expected her to hiss, "Big horse!" Maybe the dance was beautiful and graceful, et cetera, but it wasn't Ugly Girl's style. I whispered in Mom's ear, "I need fresh air. I'm out of here." Mom grabbed my wrist and glared at me. As if Mom could hold Ugly Girl by the wrist. "Ursula," she whispered, "I spent forty-five dollars for these tickets. You are *not leaving*." Mom's eyes showed a dangerous rim of white above the irises but Ugly Girl was already making her move. "Mom, I'll meet you guys right out front. I promise."

"Ur-sula!"

"I'm out of here."

Lisa was embarrassed of her big sister, or possibly ashamed. She was sitting on Mom's other side and just kept staring at the stage as I pushed and stumbled out to the aisle mumbling, "Excuse me!"

Out in the lobby, I immediately felt so *free*. Like, if I'd been a horse, a tight-fitting bridle had been removed. Now I could toss my head and *gallop*.

I checked at the box office to see when the dance let out, and actually did go running across the windy plaza at Lincoln Centre in the direction of Central Park. My boots weren't the best for running, but they'd have to do. As soon as I got to the park, on the snowy grass, I could run better. I was trotting, my breath steaming in the cold air. Not that it was very cold, just below freezing. A glowering midwinter day. I watched the skaters for a while. I walked around the big pond. I could *breathe*. Mom didn't like me to wander around alone in the city, but I never felt in any danger, that was the advantage of being Ugly Girl at five feet ten and a half inches tall. (In fact, in these boots, five feet eleven.) Especially in the park on a sunny Sunday afternoon I felt safe.

I had lots of time. I went to an art exhibit at the National Academy of Design. The posters out front intrigued me: PEN-AND-INK MASTERS. I hadn't been drawing much lately, since quitting basketball and my sour feeling about school and Inky Black moods sort of gripping me, so it was exciting to see this exhibit of drawings by older artists like Rembrandt, Matisse, Degas, Picasso, and Dürer (who I'd never heard of before but who was the best, with fantastic drawings of rabbits and birds more real than "real" that made me just want to stare for long minutes) and more recent artists, like R B Kitaj, Alice Neel, Anne Dunn, Joan Mitchell, Jane Freilicher... It was exciting to see women artists mixed with men, even if their names didn't mean too much to me. Their art was *good.* I was feeling inspired again, and couldn't wait to get home to my sketch pad. And in the book shop I picked up *The Obstacle Race: The Fortunes of Women Painters and Their Work* by Germaine Greer, who I'd sort of heard of, and leafed through it, and this leaped out at me:

> More insidious than the teachers' contempt was their praise. At all the art schools women consistently bore off the honours... Women easily confused this kind of success with genuine artistic achievement. In such a situation it is very likely that the wrong women were encouraged, for true artistic ability often presents itself in a truculent aspect which does not find favour with paternalist teachers.

These words really struck me. It was like the author was talking directly to Ugly Girl. It was worth coming to New York just to read this.

*Truculent:* I was pretty sure I knew what the word meant, and it meant Ugly Girl.

Then, crossing through the park to return to Lincoln Centre, I had a shock.

This sensation went through me swift as an electric current. I stopped to watch the skaters again and I saw – I thought I saw – a familiar-looking tall lanky boy with faded-red hair and a pale freckled skin, skating in flashy figure eights. He was showing off for a girl, and they were both wearing red gloves.

I stopped dead in my tracks and stared.

Matt Donaghy?

Matt Donaghy here in Central Park, skating with a girl?

My mouth went dry. My heart began to beat strangely. I wanted to shrink away to hide before Matt saw me, but at the same time (this was crazy, for sure) I wanted to step into view and capture Matt's attention.

*Hey. I'm your friend. Ursula Riggs. Me.*

The red-haired boy and his girlfriend joined hands and skated away as if to mock me. Other skaters blocked my view. My eyes blurred with moisture so I had to rub them clear to see, when the couple came back into view – no, of course the boy wasn't Matt Donaghy.

He was a total stranger, older than Matt. Not so nice-looking as Matt, with a hard face.

Ugly Girl hurried away, blushing.

This was not good.

I had to hurry now, I was almost late to meet up with Mom and Lisa. And I knew Mom was seriously pissed at me.

On Broadway there were these tough-looking girls, a few years older than me, in sexy leather pants and funky little jackets, their spiky hair dyed in streaks of green, maroon, orange, and their earlobes pierced and glittering like mine. Except they wore nose rings too. Were they *cool!* Seeing me, they whistled. "Hey there, sexy!" They were grinning and waving. I smiled back but didn't say anything, feeling shy. I kept walking.

Still, it felt good. They were Ugly Girls too.

# SEVENTEEN

**Winter loneliness. Winter** solitude. You could drift away into the hilly, rock-strewn woods and feel your body begin to lose its heat and turn to stone. There you wouldn't have to hear your mother and father talking, murmuring, their voices occasionally raised and angry in the night.

You wouldn't have to hear voices at school lowered in your presence. You wouldn't have to see the covert glances.

*Poor Matt. He's changed so much...*

*He isn't much fun any more, is he?*

Mr Rainey wanted Matt to make an appointment to see him. Just to talk. But Matt had nothing to say to Mr Rainey, so why make an appointment "just to talk"?

More and more Matt was going hiking in the preserve without taking Pumpkin. Why? The golden retriever whimpered to Matt at the door, practically begging him to take her, but Matt had his reasons. "No. This is private. Next time, Pumpkin."

If ever Matt wanted to turn into stone, to stop his racing thoughts and the edgy nervous sensation like ticks crawling over his skin, Pumpkin would just interfere.

Matt came in from a hike, and there was Alex in the kitchen, looking frightened. "Where's Mom?" Matt asked. It was a Sunday in February, a few minutes before noon. Matt's dad was in Houston, or maybe it was Dallas. San Diego?

Without Dad in the house, the tension was lessened. Usually.

Alex was saying, "Mom was going through yesterday's mail and opened something... She's in the bathroom." Matt listened at the bathroom door and heard the fan whirring inside, and the sound of sobbing. "Hey, Mom?" Matt rapped shyly on the door. "Are you – OK?"

Stupid question. How could Mom be OK, hiding in a bathroom crying?

Alex said, "It came in this, I guess." On top of a small pile of mail was a plain white envelope with no return address. MR & MRS DONAGHY, 377 GLENDALE DR, ROCKY RIVER, NY was scrawled on it in oversized letters, in red ink.

Matt was impatient with his brother standing there gaping. "Go away, Alex. Mom needs privacy." Alex's face showed surprise at the harshness of Matt's voice, but he turned to leave. "And take Pumpkin with you, will you? She's getting on my nerves."

"She's your dog, Matt."

But Alex took Pumpkin, running upstairs to his room.

When Matt's mother finally emerged from the bathroom,

he was shocked at her appearance. Her face looked smudged, her eyes were bloodshot. Her hands shook. "I can't take this any longer," she said. "I'm exhausted." Matt wasn't accustomed to his mother in this state, unapologetic for her tears. This scared him as much as anything.

"Mom, what is it? Did somebody—"

"This."

She handed him a newspaper clipping. It was an article Matt had already seen, taken from a Westchester paper the previous month; the headline was AREA TEEN QUESTIONED IN BOMB SCARE. Beside the headline were question marks in red. Someone had scrawled in block letters:

YOUR NEIGHBOURS ARE NOT SAFE
WE ARE NOT GOING TO FORGET

Matt's mother was saying, in a flat, tired voice Matt had never before heard, that she wanted to move away from Rocky River. She wasn't happy here any longer. She didn't feel safe. None of them were safe. "I go into the food market, into the drugstore, and I can see people looking at me. I know. The cashiers stare at me. Some of them know me from... before. They try to be nice. A few of them have even expressed sympathy. The same with our neighbours. Our so-called friends. But still, I'm 'Mrs Donaghy the mother of the boy who was arrested – you know, the bomb-scare boy'." Matt's mother spoke bitterly, imitating another's voice. Her mouth twisted in a way ugly to witness. "We can't stay here. I used to love this house; now I hate it! There's too much glass in this house. Look

– those windows." Matt looked, and saw just the driveway and the snowy backyard. Only at night, when their lights were on, could you see signs of a neighbouring house. "I'm telling your father tonight. We aren't safe!"

Matt stood tall and gangly and awkward, not knowing what to do. He wanted to hug his mother, to comfort her, but that felt wrong – Mom was the one who hugged Matt when he was upset.

Mom was the one who didn't cry. Once she'd hurt herself playing tennis, twisting an ankle, and she was crying but at the same time laughing to assure her family she was fine. She was all right! If Matt or Alex was angry, or sullen, or hurt, Mom was the one to cajole him out of it. She used sympathy, or she used humour. Always, Mom knew what to do. It was a shock to Matt that his mom was speaking so frankly to him, as if he were an adult. It was a shock to see her face: raw and exposed. And her eyes accusing.

Matt would have torn the clipping into pieces except his mother stopped him. "This is for your father to see. He needs to know."

"Mom, I—"

"He needs to know! He's gone all the time – none of this is real enough to him. We're not real to him – enough."

Matt tried to joke, "Maybe we're too real to him, Mom. Maybe I am."

But Matt's mother wasn't in a joking mood. She brushed past him, rubbing her reddened eyes with her fingertips. For a fleeting second she swayed on her feet as if she'd lost her balance.

"I'm going to lie down, Matt. I'm exhausted. It's only noon! It feels like night."

"Mom, I – I'm sorry."

"Yes. You've said."

"My big mouth—"

"We've gone over it enough, Matt. I'm tired. I'm going to lie down, Matt."

"Mom, I—"

Helplessly, Matt watched his mother walk away. Pulses in his head were pounding. Wasn't Mom going to reassure him, as she'd done so many times, that it wasn't his fault?

Wasn't she going to assure Matt that she and Daddy loved him, and believed him, and would protect him from all harm?

# EightEEN

*Truculent.* I looked up the word in the dictionary and it meant what I'd thought it meant.

I liked the sound of it, too.

*Ugly Girl, truculent warrior-woman.*

I saw Matt Donaghy in homeroom and in our class. He didn't smile and call out, "Hi, Ursula!" any longer. He didn't seem to talk to many people any longer. He didn't smile much. When Mr Weinberg asked his enigmatic questions, Matt didn't quickly raise his hand to answer as he used to. I felt bad about this, and I could tell that Mr Weinberg felt bad too. It's like Matt was fading away, in our presence. I'd heard about him resigning his class office and quitting the school newspaper, and he sat by himself at lunch instead of with his old clique, or didn't have lunch at school at all. I wanted to talk to him but didn't know how. My mouth went dry, my heart hammered just at the thought. *Hi Matt. How are things going... ?* It was all so banal and predictable, I just couldn't. Ugly Girl scorned idiotic small talk.

Especially with a guy.

I'd sent Matt an e-mail message, that time. Maybe I could send him a message again?

I tried, and tried. My brain went blank. I just couldn't.

Since they'd pushed me on the stairs, it seemed I kept seeing the Brewer twins around school. Of the hundreds of kids at Rocky River, if there was one individual you didn't want to see, that's the one you saw. In this case, two.

It seemed to be by accident, because Muriel and Miriam never looked happy to see me. They looked almost scared, or were pretending to be scared. Like they were afraid Ugly Girl might rush over and punch them in their smirky faces.

Mostly I ignored them. I was good at ignoring insult.

*Jew-girl. Jew-girl!*

I knew they were mouthing this. I wanted to laugh and call after them – "Sure, I'm a Jew! And I'm proud of it."

But one day it dawned on me: they were the ones.

Of course! Muriel and Miriam Brewer.

I tracked them down in the senior corridor and said accusingly, "*You* did it, didn't you? You two. You reported Matt Donaghy to Mr Parrish, *and you lied.*"

I saw by the guilty expressions on their pale faces that I was correct. But they were such cowards, they denied it. One shook her head, backing away. "We did not. *That's* a lie." The other said defiantly, "Reported who? We don't know what you're talking about."

"You informed on Matt Donaghy. You lied, and got him into trouble." I was getting more and more excited, now I knew I was correct. "It was you two, wasn't it! The 'witnesses'."

One of the twins said, "No! We did not. We don't have to talk to you." The other said, turning her lower lip out again, in that way that made me want to hit her, "Our father says we don't have to answer any questions. We're protected by the law."

"What law? A law to protect liars?"

Suddenly they both began shouting. "He did too say those things! We heard him! We went right home and told our father, and he called the office here – and he called the police. That's our duty as citizens."

I said, "You were lying! You never heard what you said you heard."

"We did too. *We did too.*"

It was just following the last class of the day. Lots of people were trooping out, and this exchange was being overheard. I saw Ms Zwilich, and she was just standing there, a few yards away, her jaw practically dropping. The Brewer twins! Why would anyone have believed *them*? They were saying, in mocking voices, "You can't prove it, you can't prove anything. We were not lying, we told the truth." I was advancing upon these two like they were arrogant guards on the opposing team and I had the basketball and was bouncing it rapid-fire like a machine gun. If they stayed between me and my goal, I'd run them right over.

They didn't, though. They fled.

# NINETEEN

Everybody at Rocky River High was buzzing.

Two new, startling developments.

The first was met with shock and incredulity, in some quarters even disgust.

"The Brewer twins? They were the ones?"

"Gosh, who'd believe *them*?"

It had become general knowledge that Muriel and Miriam Brewer were the mystery witnesses who'd informed on Matt Donaghy.

"Muriel and Miriam! That is so *weird*."

"Everybody knows they're crazy."

"They're not crazy, they're mean."

"It isn't them, my mom says. It's their father. Reverend 'Ike'."

"But who'd believe them? Any of the Brewers?"

"Mr Parrish must've. He called the cops."

Within a few hours the story had developed that Muriel Brewer – unless it was Miriam – or maybe both? – had had a "serious crush" on Matt Donaghy and Matt had snubbed her, or them. "That's the reason for Muriel and Miriam taking revenge. If one twin wants to do something, the other always helps."

Next morning the story had become more complicated. Now Ursula Riggs was somehow involved.

"Wow! Big Ursula."

"She stuck up for Matt Donaghy with Mr Parrish and the cops. She practically punched out the Brewers."

"Ursula Riggs! She's weird."

"Ursula's cool."

"I never knew Ursula and Matt Donaghy were friends..."

"Since when? Are they?"

"Nobody's ever seen them together... have they?"

"Matt's tall enough."

"Matt isn't *big* enough."

They lowered their voices, laughing together. This was all so weird, it was kind of wonderful.

"...except you're forgetting one thing."

"What?"

"Big Ursula hates men."

The second development was equally shocking.

"They're *suing*? The Donaghys?"

"They're suing Mr Parrish, and the school, and the school district, and the Brewers. For twenty or thirty million dollars, I heard."

"*I* heard fifty million. At least."

"They're charging 'defamation of character'. 'Mental cruelty' – something like that."

"'Mental distress.'"

"*I* wouldn't mind 'mental distress' for that kind of money."

Within a few hours the story had developed that the Donaghys were claiming they'd received "death threats" – and Matt Donaghy was "seeing a shrink" – "an expensive New York shrink, who specialises in 'disturbed adolescent boys'." They were suing for $100 million!

"Hell, I don't blame them. Matt's a good guy, and he's had to put up with some serious crap over this."

"Not a hundred million dollars' worth!"

"It's over now – the Donaghys should put it behind them."

"'Forget and forgive.' Right."

They were talking loudly, indignantly. Upstairs in the junior corridor outside Mr Weinberg's homeroom. (Did they hope that Matt Donaghy, quietly shutting his locker at the far end of the corridor, slipping on his backpack, and walking quickly to the back stairs, might overhear?)

Mr Weinberg appeared, carrying a briefcase that tugged at his arm as if it were weighted down with bricks. The popular English and drama teacher was unsmiling and looked tired; even his moustache drooped.

"Mr Weinberg? What do you think about the Donaghys suing us?"

Mr Weinberg, who usually responded to questions with a quick wisecrack, frowned and said, shrugging, "No comment, kids."

"It's a lousy idea, huh? It's just gonna make things worse."

Mr Weinberg continued towards the stairs. Over his shoulder he said, "Kids, I said no comment."

"Are *you* being sued, Mr Weinberg?"

"Better get a lawyer, Mr Weinberg!"

But Mr Weinberg was gone.

"He's against it, you can tell."

"It's a terrible mistake. Matt shouldn't let his folks do it."

"It's just gonna get in the papers, and on TV. More reporters coming around."

"The Donaghys should put this mess behind them, like we all did. 'Forget and forgive'."

"'Forgive and forget.'"

"Whatever."


Ursula Riggs was shutting her locker. She turned to see three or four juniors standing indecisively a few yards away, as if they had something to ask and were steeling up the nerve.

Ursula scowled at them. "Yes? What?"

"Ursula, what do you think—"

"—about the Donaghys suing the school?"

Ursula's big-boned face darkened with blood, and her eyes narrowed. She jammed the soiled Mets cap on her head. "That's their business."

"But – do you think it's a good idea, or – not?"

"I said that's their business."

They watched Ursula Riggs stomp off. *She* was a character. Today she was wearing a man's white cotton long-sleeved shirt, buttoned at the cuffs, hanging loose and baggy over her rumpled khakis, and badly water-stained running shoes. And studs glittering in her ears. The daughter of Clayton Riggs, who'd believe it? And Ursula's mother was a normal, attractive Rocky River wife, and her kid sister, Lisa, was a normal, pretty girl. Who could figure Big Ursula?

This new rumour about Ursula Riggs and Matt Donaghy was so ridiculous, you almost wished it might be true.

# tWENty

**There it Was:** Matt Donaghy's empty desk, in homeroom. Three rows to my left, two desks back. From the corner of my eye I saw it was empty. And in Mr Weinberg's class Matt's desk was also empty.

I kept being distracted, during classes. Wondering...

No. I was relieved Matt wasn't around. I wouldn't have to see him.

People were making snide remarks, of course. Even his friends. (Ex-friends?) Sure, they felt sorry for him – but. And the jocks, who pretended to love ol' Rocky River HS, were talking of Matt Donaghy as a "traitor" – and worse.

(The worst thing to call a guy, in jockese, is "fag". You hear that a lot. Must be something about that syllable that really turns those guys on, right?)

I missed Matt Donaghy. That empty seat. Like he'd moved... or died.

Which was weird because, if Matt had been in school, Ugly Girl would've ignored him anyway.

I guess.

"More trouble at that school of yours, Ursula! Now lawyers are involved. Ouch!" It was Dad, reading the front-page article in the *Westchester Journal.* ROCKY RIVER SCHOOL DISTRICT PRIME TARGET OF $50 MILLION DEFAMATION SUIT. It was sort of shocking to see the name *Donaghy* in print for the first time. *Claire and William Donaghy,* plaintiffs. *Matthew Donaghy,* 16, their son. Now Matt's name was right there in the paper, and would be on TV and radio, and it would be worse for him than before.

I didn't think it was such a hot idea. Asking for money made everything so cheap somehow. Maybe Mr Parrish overreacted, but he wasn't a bad guy, for a principal. Maybe the Brewers deserved it, though. Nobody'd ever brought a lawsuit against Reverend "Ike" until now. Dad laughed but was shaking his head. He'd had some really bad experiences with multimillion-dollar lawsuits, not personally but in business. "You'd think the Donaghys would want to put this mess behind them, wouldn't you?"

I said, "It's their business what they want to do, Dad."

"How does the boy feel about it?"

This made me really flare up. A Fiery Red right up my spine.

"Dad, I'm not a friend of Matt Donaghy's, you know that."

"Tell your friend Matt, free advice from Clay Riggs, this is a big mistake. Whatever the school district settles, however it turns out, the guys to profit will be you know who."

Lawyers, Dad meant. But I wasn't listening to this. My face was burning and I was halfway out the door.

# tWENty-ONE

"HEy, DONagh-y!"

"Hey, fag!"

"You hear us, Donaghy! Don't pretend you don't."

Matt heard. Matt had seen them approaching, from the corner of his eye. He'd been hearing their voices. Their sniggering laughter. He didn't look around, and he didn't acknowledge them. It was probably hopeless, but he began to walk faster.

"Hey, fag, what's the hurry?"

"Where're you going in such a hurry, fag?"

Should he run? He was a good runner for short sprints, less good at distances. Two of the guys behind him were football players, which meant they'd be good at moderate distances and strong when they hit him. Matt's heart was beginning to pound hard, pumping adrenaline. Run!

He was headed for the steps at the end of the alley. A flight of concrete steps leading down to an asphalt parking lot below Main Street. The narrow alley was between the Rocky River Shoe Repair and Bon Appetite Gourmet Foods, a shortcut to the parking lot. Matt had been running errands for his mother, who wasn't well. It was a few days after the news of the lawsuit had been reported locally, and Matt knew when he saw the boys from Rocky River High following him that there'd be trouble.

The boys were mostly seniors, outweighing Matt by twenty or more pounds. Trevor Cassity, Duane Stanton, Rod Booth and two or three others. He knew them from school – in the cafeteria especially they'd been taunting him.

Making sucking noises with their mouths. "'Sue me!' C'mon – 'sue me!' Fag."

Matt was going to run for the steps, but there was Duane Stanton blocking his way. He hesitated and felt a hand grab roughly at his shoulder, and at his backpack. He clenched his fist, swung at them blindly. This was happening so swiftly, it was impossible to see. His hand recoiled in pain. He'd struck Cassity on the side of the head. Cassity grunted in surprise and struck back. One of the others hit Matt a stunning blow on the jaw. The older, bigger boys were dancing around Matt, jeering, grinning. Like a hyena pack. Matt was panting and frightened, yet would recall afterwards how strangely calm he was. *This is what you deserve. Big Mouth. You know it is.* His nose had begun to bleed. The front of his windbreaker would be stained. There were more punches thrown, some of them missing their target. The struggle wasn't graceful or coordinated, like a boxing match or a fight scene in a movie. Matt ducked, and kicked at his opponents, who laughed angrily, jeered, even spat at him. They were calling him names, obscenities. He did not know why they hated him so much – or whether they hated him at all but were only attacking him for sport. "So what're you gonna do, sue us?" – "Sue us?" – "Fag, gonna sue us?" One of them ripped off Matt's backpack and threw it down the concrete steps, Matt lost his balance reaching for it, or was tripped – and next thing he knew, he was falling sidelong down the concrete steps. His arms flailed. He tried to grab on to the railing, but it was rusted and wobbly and couldn't hold his weight. He fell, hard. He slid to the foot of the steps, a distance of about fifteen feet, and landed in chunks of ice and gritty snow.

The boys ran away laughing. But their mocking words echoed in Matt's head. *Sue us – sue us – sue us!*

# tWENty-twO

That WEEk I was in a Fiery Red mood. At least I was feeling pretty good about my drawing again: charcoal sketches and pen and ink. And a high grade (99 per cent) in biology lab. Ms Schultz was on speaking terms with me again, and (I guessed) I was on speaking terms with her. And some of the girls on the team, including Bonnie, who was my friend anyway, were behaving friendly, sort of, towards Ugly Girl.

I had to admit, I was missing the games. Without a team sport there's a hole in your life.

This weird thing: there was Ms Schultz and one of the girls on the team talking together in the hall, and it flashed through me that when they saw me, they were going to smile and call out, "Hi, Ursula!" and maybe wave me over, and it flashed through me I couldn't trust myself not to be emotional, so I turned away pretending I hadn't seen them and got the hell out of there fast.

It was like Ugly Girl was spinning out of control. Even for Ugly Girl.

At home, things were weird too. Mom was giving me the cool, hurt, silent treatment, as if Ugly Girl was somebody's daughter who gave a damn about such tactics. Mom was waiting for me to apologise for my "atrocious behaviour" at Lincoln Centre, I guess.

Well, I wasn't going to apologise. I was thinking I would never apologise for anything again in my life that, when I did it, felt right.

What surprised me, though, was how Lisa was starting to behave.

My sister wasn't even twelve, and almost it seemed she was beginning to be aggressive with *me*.

I'd try to tease her like I always did. Saying things like "Hey Lisa, how's your *bale-lay* lessons?" but she would stiffen like I'd poked her a little too hard, wouldn't even look at me, or she'd whisper, "Leave me alone. I hate you."

Well. I knew Lisa didn't mean it.

*I hate you.* That hurt, kind of.

In the beginning, when Lisa started dance lessons, she'd been a little girl, maybe four years old. All the little girls taking lessons were so cute, and it seemed innocent enough, "training" them like real dancers. But within the last two years I'd noticed a real change in Lisa. The dance lessons weren't just about dancing but about competition. No matter how good you were, some other girl was possibly better. The nightmare was, in a troupe of struggling girls, one girl had to be the least talented. One girl, maybe, had to be just a little "overweight".

It scared me that Lisa was going through what I'd gone through on the swim team.

Every few months it seemed girls were dropping out of Lisa's class, feeling like failures at eleven or twelve. I'd overhear Mom and Lisa eagerly discussing who was in, who was out. I hated how edgy and anxious it was making them both, and I told them so.

There she was, my little sister, pushing food around on her plate like it was poison. Like she had a dread of gaining a pound on her flimsy sparrow bones. And Mom wasn't noticing? I said, "Lisa, what the hell? Are you *dieting*?" making *dieting* sound like something really stupid, and Lisa didn't look at me but muttered, "No, I am not. *You* should." (Which was the first time, ever, that Lisa said anything like that to me.) And Mom got into it quick, saying, "Ursula, leave your sister alone. You're always picking on her." And I shot back, "If Lisa becomes anorexic, Mom, it's going to be *your fault.*" And both of them turned on me then, practically beating Ugly Girl back with sticks.

I saw they were allies in this. Like it was the two of them against me.

I just laughed. Took my dinner upstairs on a tray, to eat alone.

Dad was in Tokyo, or maybe Bangkok, and couldn't be home for dinner anyway.

In my room I read in that art book about women artists, by Germaine Greer, I'd discovered in New York. This copy I borrowed from the Rocky River Public Library, and I resolved I would buy a copy of my own.

The "obstacle race", the author called it: trying to maintain your own integrity and your own talent, no matter how others tried to influence you. Germaine Greer was talking mostly about how men oppressed women, but, I could see, women and girls did it to themselves, too.

Why?

Sure, I'd been thinking about Matt Donaghy, too.

Next day, a Saturday, I had to get out of the house.

The nature preserve was less than a mile from our house. Something was drawing me there – I could almost feel it.

The preserve was about forty acres, and a lot of it was hilly. Most people used the shorter trails closer to the roads. There were hiking trails marked .5 mile, 2 miles, etc. My favourite was Windy Point Trail, which was five miles, almost too hilly and rock-strewn for winter, when ice covered shale outcroppings and made hiking dangerous. But you could go a couple of miles on this trail, where it ran beside the Rocky River Creek.

The creek was so beautiful, I thought. Frozen at its banks into lacy ice patterns but clear and fast running in the middle.

Just chance I took Windy Point. Or maybe I had a premonition.

# tWENty-thrEE

**Nobody would know!** *Nobody could even guess.*
*Turning into stone... and no one can hurt you.*

"Pumpkin, no. Sorry, girl – you're staying home today."

The golden retriever peered up at Matt with her moist, yearning eyes. I love you! Why can't I go with you? What's wrong? What's wrong with *you*?

Matt rubbed the dog's furry bony head, stroked her soft ears, scratched behind her ears. He was feeling guilty, which was ridiculous. Pumpkin loved him no matter what. "See, I'm just not in a happy mood, Pumpkin. You're too optimistic for me."

If something happened to Matt Donaghy, they'd search in the preserve. They'd send Pumpkin after him. Sniffing eagerly along the trail. Barking, whimpering. Like a scene in a sentimental TV movie. Matt didn't want to think about it, and erased it from his mind as he was erasing so much now.

Like Mom's sobbing in the bathroom. Dad's voice raised on the telephone. Alex's hurt eyes, turning away from Matt.

Like the front-page articles in the local papers. DEFAMATION. $50 MILLION. ROCKY RIVER RESIDENTS INITIATE LAWSUIT. Like Matt's friends – his former friends – avoiding him, and those who didn't avoid him, Denis Wheeler for instance, trying so hard to be nice to him, Matt had to be the one to shake Denis off, saying curtly, "Thanks, Denis. But I don't need your charity. That's an insult to me." (Matt was trembling with some weird emotion he couldn't recognise. He wanted to laugh in Denis's surprised, hurt face. He liked it that Denis would spread the word among his friends. *Matt Donaghy doesn't want our charity.*)

Most of all Matt wanted to erase the memory of Cassity, Stanton, Booth and the other Rocky River jocks jeering at him, shoving and punching. "Fag!" – "So? Gonna sue us, fag?" No one had ever hit Matt like that. So deliberately, purposefully. Wanting to hurt him. Really wanting to hurt him. As if they'd forgotten that Matt hadn't wanted to blow up the school and shoot people, was innocent of that charge. *You deserve this, Big Mouth.* They'd knocked him down the steps and run away laughing. Things like this didn't happen in Rocky River. At the bottom of the concrete steps Matt lay in the gritty snow trying not to cry, bleeding from his nose. A woman parking her car discovered him and helped him stand, wiped at his face with tissues, offered to drive him to the medical centre, but Matt insisted he'd just slipped and fallen from a few steps up. He hadn't fallen far, and he wasn't hurt. "Are you sure?" the woman asked doubtfully. She was Matt's mother's age; he was grateful she didn't know him.

All these things Matt meant to erase just by hiking in the preserve on this windy blue day.

*Erase. Delete. Exit.*

*Are you sure? Y/N.*

*Y.*

"I love it here. I could die here... and be happy."

The township of Rocky River was misnamed, for the body of water that ran through it was a creek, not a river. Rocky River Creek was maybe one hundredth the width of the Hudson River and no more than five or six feet deep at its deepest. It flowed down in a westerly direction into the Hudson, in a twisty, boulder-strewn stream bed, out of the hills of Rockefeller State Park. The creek was often nearly dry in summer and overflowed its banks in rainy seasons. Early settlers on this eastern bank of the Hudson River had named their fur-trading post Rocky River in the 1600s. All was wilderness then. Now there was an unbroken string of suburban villages, most of them affluent, on the river, linked by Route 9 descending south into Manhattan. Rocky River was situated between Briarcliff Manor and Tarrytown, a half-hour train ride to midtown Manhattan, the most expensive real estate in the world.

Matt started up the trail beside the boulder-strewn creek. He knew the trail well, but it was icy in winter, and you had to be careful not to slip. It was a good feeling – his heart beginning to beat harder, and his leg muscles pulling. And his breath steamed. It was so terrific here! This was his place; he was happy here. Storm clouds at the horizon, but much of the sky a clear hard blue. Arctic blue. The wind was picking up – maybe it would blow the clouds away. Matt didn't care. Maybe it would snow, there'd be a snowstorm. He'd be authentically lost. No one could blame him. An accident.

Outside the preserve there was a Nothing-World.

Outside the preserve there were only Nothing-Days waiting.

Matt missed Pumpkin trotting and sniffing in the woods, peeing on rocks, logs, chunks of ice, with that comical-thoughtful doggy expression. As if thinking, *Peeing is my duty, I don't know why. So I'd better do it.*

By nature Pumpkin was a retriever, a hunting dog. Matt used to feel guilty that he wasn't a hunter, that the most he could do for Pumpkin was toss sticks and Frisbees for her to retrieve, and that quickly became boring.

Pumpkin would miss Matt. If he failed to return. Matt felt a stab of guilt... but no. Alex could love Pumpkin enough for them both. Alex was a smart, sweet kid.

"He'll understand."

The boulders were icy but partly wet. Shimmering in the sun. Matt stared. He felt he could be hypnotised by the cascading water. So cold! The creek was frozen at its edges, a stark frost white, but thawed in the middle as that dark water rushed downwards. The wind was picking up. His nose was running. There was something he was trying to think of.... He was very tired suddenly. He wanted to lie down. No, he wanted to climb into that ravine and up its steep farther bank. Why, he couldn't have said. Everywhere were boulders and rocks and pebbles. He loved a stony place. He lost his footing, almost fell, grabbed on to a boulder. If Pumpkin was here, she'd be sniffing around, peeing and trotting and glancing back at Matt to see where he was, how he was. Keeping him in view. She'd be leading him, except she'd circle back to follow him. Maybe they were hunting? But hunting what? Matt was determined to get to the top of that ravine. His boots were slipping. He clutched at – what? A tree limb that broke off in his hand.

Still, he was determined. He wasn't going to give up.

# tWENty-four

"Matt?"

I saw him, and I knew it was him. I recognised his dark-green windbreaker. A green knit cap on his head. Matt Donaghy.

What was Matt doing? Crouched there on the edge of a cliff just staring down at the rushing water... like he's hypnotised.

That look in his face. Preparing for something. What?

"Matt? Hey."

Now he had to hear me – I'd raised my voice pretty loud. I made a lot of noise hiking up the trail behind him, deliberately. To wake him. He was blinking at me. As if it took a few seconds to recognise me, or to realise where he was.

He began to stammer. "Ursula? What – are you doing here?"

"This is one of my places. I'm always here."

I spoke quickly, and smiled. It was a swift Ugly Girl tactic to smile when you're scared as hell.

Had Matt been about to jump? "Slip" on the icy rocks and fall into that ravine? It was about thirty feet down. Big boulders, and through the centre, like a razor-blade cut, that dark cascading water.

Should I let Matt know I'd seen? *And I knew?*

There wasn't time to think, much. I was scared and nervous, and my adrenaline was pumping like in a game, when you could lose, or you could win, depending upon your strategy.

I kept approaching Matt, off the trail now and climbing the hill. It was tough going. It was dangerous. I'm not the kind of outdoor type who does reckless things, like rock climbing without the right gear. You could say that Ugly Girl was savvy as a pro for her young age, but there I was practically stumbling and crawling up this ridiculous icy-rocky hill where, even in good weather, there was no trail. I said with a big smile, like one of the Personality-Plus girls at Rocky River who think it's their duty to spread sweetness and light among the underprivileged, "Yeah! I really love it here! This creek. It's kind of a secret place. Up here in the winter... nobody's around, much."

Matt's face was pale, like he was going to be sick. His freckles looked bleached out. He looked scared, too, but he was trying to smile. He looked like a sleepwalker wakened in a place puzzling to him but trying not to let on. He said in this weird slow voice like every word had to be considered, "I... didn't know... you were here, Ursula. I..."

"Yeah, like I said. I'm here a lot."

Matt squinted at me as if he didn't trust me, clambering up the hill towards him. But he couldn't seem to think of the right thing to say, to make me stop.

My voice got brighter and brighter. Like a nurse's. Like my mom greeting guests for a dinner party she's been anxious about for days, but you'd never have guessed that now. I was saying whatever came into my head – "It's really nice to run into you here, Matt" – "We could hike together sometime, OK?" – "Why don't you come down from there, though. It's icy and dangerous and you could fall."

Matt nodded dazedly. Typical Rocky River upbringing, it's your instinct to be polite in just about any circumstances. Still, the guy was stubborn, he wouldn't move.

"Matt, like I said – it's kind of icy there, those rocks, OK? Matt, come *on.*"

Matt was listening. But still he was crouched at the edge of the ravine.

"Know what? – We could hike together. Right now. I know some cool places. Sort of secret places. A perch like an eagle's nest where you can stand and see the river, and across the river. Matt? OK?"

I was almost pleading now. This went on for five minutes, maybe. But it seemed a lot longer. I was so scared, Ugly Girl seemed to have departed. It was just me, Ursula. Talking to Matt Donaghy I'd gone to school with for years in Rocky River but didn't really know well, but we were like in this movie where somebody had to save Matt from "accidentally" falling and smashing his skull on those rocks.

I could see Matt's knees tremble. I could see his jaws tighten. I could see him thinking. *Now.*

I knew: it's like diving off the high board. Your mind has to release you, give you permission. Your body wants to survive, it doesn't want to throw itself into space. Never! Your mind has to instruct you. Now. Move.

Except something changed Matt's mind, and he turned, and stepped back from the edge. Some little stones loosened and fell as he turned. He made his way down the hill, from about fifteen feet above me, slipping and sliding, that sickly-pale scared look still on his face, and I put out my gloved hand to grab his.

Matt grabbed my hand, hard.

March

# tWENty-fivE

Thurs 3/1/01        5:25 aM

Dear Ursula,

Thank you for the other day.

Your friend Matt

# tWENty-six

Dear Ursula,
I'm thinking about the other day.
The last Saturday of February.
In biology there is always a PURPOSE to things.
Nothing is "just accident".
What do you think???

Your friend Matt

Fri 3/2/01 10:47 PM

2 mars
dear matt--
yes/no/maybe
BUT einstein said god wld not play dice with the universe
SO maybe you're right, there is ALWAYS PURPOSE.

u r

Fri 3/2/01 10:51 PM

Dear Ursula,

The other day it was like, it's hard to say it was like something that had never happened before yet was very familiar like an old dream you had a lot when you were a little kid and forgot but now you have it again and remember and it scares you, it's so real, it belongs to YOU.

That was how I felt. With you. Hiking back down and not needing to talk, like there needed nothing to be said.

Your friend Matt


But for this message, quickly as he'd typed it out, Matt struck DELETE.

# tWENty-SEVEN

"Pumpkin! Hey."

It was like he'd come back from, where? – some other planet.

Ursula must be taking French, she dated her e-mail *mars* for *March*. That felt right: *mars.*

"Pumpkin, I wasn't really going to – you know. Not *really.*"

Pumpkin was kissing his hands, like she knew but she forgave him.

"No, but I wasn't, really. I – I'm not the type."

They were upstairs in Matt's room. Quickly he'd come upstairs, and quickly he'd shut the door. *Matt, is that you?* his sleepy, startled Mom might've asked, but he didn't hear.

"I mean, I wouldn't have left *you.*"

Pumpkin was making her low excited barking sound, not an actual bark, not loud or sharp enough to classify as a bark. More like a friend saying *Yeh? Yeh?* to show you he/she's listening.

"I wouldn't have left any of *this*."

Matt made a vague sweeping gesture of a kind he'd often seen his dad make, a wave of his hand meaning, like, all-of-the-world-that's-my-experience. Sometimes when he made that gesture, his dad grimaced, like he was tasting something and he couldn't decide, Is it edible? Is it poison? But Matt was smiling, actually. Pumpkin was a dog who understood smiles, she could smile herself, grin actually, grin and laugh, in the right mood. "You believe me, Pumpkin, don't you? I was coming back."

Pumpkin believed. Even if Pumpkin didn't believe, Pumpkin trusted him.

# tWENty-Eight

HE'd felt her strong fingers close around his. He'd never gripped any girl's hand like that, he'd never gripped any human being's hand like that except his mom's and his dad's and maybe his grandparents'. But that was a long time ago, like a dream he hadn't had in so long he'd mostly forgotten it.

# tWENty-NiNE

sat 3/3/01          11:03 PM

Dear Ursula,

This is going to sound really REALLY corny but I'm still thinking a
lot about the other day.

                                        Your friend Matt


                                        Sat 3/3/01 11:48 PM

3 mars

dear matt--

so why'd you snub u r yesterday/ lunch?

                                        u r


                                        Sat 3/3/01 11:54 PM

Dear Ursula,

I wanted to sit with you & your 2 friends but--I thought you were
just being "nice".

                                                        163

Hey: I did not SNUB YOU, Ursula!

                                        Your friend Matt


                              Sun 3/4/01 12:08 AM

4 mars
dear matt--
u r is never "nice"

                        u r


                              Sun 3/4/01 12:11 AM

Dear Ursula,
You are better than "nice"; you are "good". 1 individual in 1
million.

I didn't know you wanted me to sit with you at lunch.
I guess I thought, why would you?

                                        Your friend Matt


                              Sun 3/4/01 12:18 AM

Dear Ursula,
Also I meant, I just have lunch by myself now, mostly.
The "misfits" table by the trash cans. It's easier that
way.

(When I come into the cafeteria everybody is, like--WHAT'S
DONAGHY GOT IN THAT BACKPACK?)

(There's talk of the school installing metal detectors.)

If you give a sign I will join you. But if not/ if your friends don't
want me, that's OK.

Your friend Matt

Sun 3/4/01 12:29 AM

4 mars

dear matt--

u r's friends dont tell me what to do/ not to do

u r

Sun 3/4/01 12:36 AM

Dear Ursula,

I wanted to ask you the other day--about the lawsuit.
If you think it's a good/ bad idea?

Your friend Matt

Sun 3/4/01 12:49 AM

4 mars

dear matt--

its none of u r's business. i dont judge.

(i dont listen to gossip either.)

u r

Sun 3/4/01 12:52 AM

Dear Ursula,

I know you don't. That's because you are 1 individual
in 1 million.

Why I keep thinking about what happened/ did not happen in the preserve.

Why I keep thinking where I would be now/ what I would be now/ if you had not seen me, Ursula.

(Which is why I believe it could not have been ACCIDENT.).
                                                        Your friend Matt

                                        Sun 3/4/01 12:57 AM

4 mars
dear matt--
i know, i think about it too/ its scary/ so maybe/ better not think about it ok?
                                        u r

                                        Sun 3/4/01 1:00 AM

Dear Ursula,
I'm afraid to sound like such a coward/ asshole
asking you not to tell anybody? EVER?
                                                        Your friend Matt

                                        Sun 3/4/01  1:05 AM

4 mars
dear matt--
tell who what? & why?

u r can keep a secret 1,000,000 yrs/ try me.

(dont you ever get sleepy/ sleep?)

u r

Sun 3/4/01  1:07 AM

Dear Ursula,

Hey I don't mean to keep you awake, I'm sorry.

I lose track of time I guess.

Before we say good night--maybe we could go hiking
in the preserve on Sat.?

Your friend Matt

Sun 3/4/01  1:10 AM

4 mars

dear matt--

ok for sat. ridge rd. gate. 2 pm?

7 AM is wakeup for u r/ so this is GOOD NIGHT MATT.

u r

Sun 3/4/01 1:13 AM

Dear Ursula,

I will meet you Sat. at 2 PM, Ridge Rd. gate.

I will be bringing a (4-footed) friend of mine & hope you aren't
allergic to silky-haired golden retrievers.

I guess you won't read this till morning so GOOD NIGHT URSULA.

Your friend Matt

Dear Ursula,
I know you're asleep, & will read this in the morning.
I don't mind being awake.

My mind just runs, runs, RUNS RUNS RUNS.

(Pumpkin, my golden retriever, sleeps like a puppy. She's not
supposed to be on my bed, but.)

I was trying to remember when we were first in school together.
Third grade, Rocky River Elementary?

I wonder what would have happened if you had not spoken
to Mr Parrish & the detectives. Maybe by this time Big Mouth
would be in jail.

Or worse.

Your friend Matt

Sun 3/4/01 3:40 AM

Dear Ursula,

I was almost asleep then my mind clicked back on. I wanted to
say to you--if you think the lawsuit my dad & mom are bringing
against people is wrong, will you tell me?

You would not say anything false, I know. There are few girls like you at Rocky River. (Few guys, either!) Everybody is so PHONY.

(That's a cliche, I know. Calling other people PHONY. Nobody's PHONIER than a Big Mouth.)

Maybe we'll have lunch today?

It's funny about sleep. I used to sleep 10 hours at a stretch, my mom would tease she was worried I was turning into a sloth. Now I sleep 3 or 4 hours a night, no more. Some nights I don't even bother to get undressed, just lie on my bed. I don't turn out the light. I try to write, or do homework, but my head isn't too clear. But I can play chess with "XO", my friend (I have never met) in Nome, Alaska.

(Do you have on-line friends? I do. I don't know who they are really. My parents are worried about "paedophiles on the Internet". I have friends in New Zealand, Hawaii, Scotland, Canada, plus the US. They don't know "Matt Donaghy". I'm happiest in cyberspace. Or was.)

If Dad's home & notices I'm still up he might knock on my door & say I should get to sleep. Tonight he isn't home, though.

Mom gave me some of her barbiturate pills "to help with your insomnia" but they made me feel like my head was clogged with phlegm. I flushed them down the toilet. (Mom takes Prozac too, or something like Prozac. I heard her say, of her friends, there's nobody NOT on some antidepressant.) Guys on the teams taking steroids. I REFUSE TO GIVE IN.

In school sometimes I'm wide awake but I start to nod off. Like the teacher and everybody else melts into a dream. When the detectives were questioning me, over & over the same questions, it was like that. Sometimes I "heard" my voice say something I didn't know was actual, or just in my head.

(I never told anybody this, Ursula. When they came to get me in study period, & began to question me, there was a look between them: they thought [maybe] I'd murdered my mother. Until they called her & heard her voice this is a thought they had & believed me capable of. I will never forget that.)

I really liked the answer you gave when Mr W. asked about Gatsby: is he a hero to take the blame for a crime somebody else did, because he loves her, or is he a fool? You said, "A hero can be a fool, he's still a hero." That's the coolest answer. Mr W. was impressed I could tell.

HE doesn't think the lawsuit is a good idea. He isn't my friend any longer anyway.

My parents have made an appointment for me to see a shrink next week. Not Mr Rainey, they don't trust anybody at RRHS now. (The school staff will be giving "depositions" for the defence. My parents are worried there might be things in my record that will be used against me.)

The shrink is a Park Ave. psychiatrist recommended by somebody Mom knows whose daughter tried to kill herself freshman year at Harvard. I overhear Mom & Dad talking about me a lot. Like I have become this disease they have, like leprosy. The shrink wrote a best-selling book I found in their bedroom-- ADOLESCENTS AT RISK: YOUR CHILD AND DEPRESSION. I opened the book to a chapter titled "Teenaged Suicide in America" & drew a happy face-- :-)

I figure if my parents get that far reading the book, they will need to be cheered up.

I hope, about the lawsuit, YOU WILL TELL ME WHAT YOU THINK.

It isn't just the $$$. My dad says winning a lawsuit is the only kind of JUSTICE people in our position can hope for. Because what was done to me wasn't a "crime". It can only be brought to civil court. There, you can demand money for being treated like shit.

Maybe you still feel like shit. But you can be "compensated" for it.

What really hurt was believing the Brewers. And not me. The Brewers! When everybody in Rocky River knows what Reverend Brewer is like.

My mom isn't herself any longer. She used to like her realtor job, now she has quit. She's ashamed of me, I guess. (She used to be proud.)

Her friends have stopped calling. She has this idea of sending me to a private school In Massachusetts & selling this house & moving away. (Where?)

My dad actually seems to like the lawsuit. He'd been so angry & tired & depressed but now with Mr Leacock he can talk for hours. He's hopeful as a kid. "A lawsuit is a duel," Dad says. "A fight to the finish." Rubbing his hands together & laughing. (He's looking for a new job where he can get more respect, he says. This is TOP SECRET & we never talk about it among ourselves.)

The one I feel sorry for is Alex. He's worried we'll move away, he'll lose his friends. In 5th grade he's still OK. He isn't touched by this. (I hope.) His friends are great little guys who don't know/ don't care about the lawsuit. Or me. Alex is a good kid I feel I am being a very bad model for, & betraying.

I'm so tired of EXPLAINING MYSELF to everybody. You're the only one who never asks questions, Ursula. You just seem to know.

It was like we'd already known each other, in the preserve. I heard this voice call--"Matt". And afterwards, hiking back down. We didn't need to talk. Like we'd done the hike lots of times together. It was so easy to be with you.

Ursula, is it OK if I call you sometime? On the phone? (I'm a little shy on the phone, I guess. But it's lonely on the computer. Not many laughs.)

Hey. I feel a lot better now. Telling you these things. & knowing you wouldn't tell anybody else, the way most girls would. It's 3:35 AM & I can't believe I actually feel sleepy.

GOOD NIGHT URSULA

Your friend Matt

# thirty

FIERY RED. I was feeling so good.

*Like we'd already known each other. In biology there is always a purpose to things. 1 individual in 1 million.*

That first week in March, Matt and I started having lunch together every day in the cafeteria. The first time I'd come into the cafeteria late and seen Matt sitting at the misfits' table by the trash cans, so I took my tray over and joined him. "Is this seat free?"

Matt stared at me for a moment without speaking. Like he was surprised to see me.

We e-mailed each other a dozen times an evening, and talked on the phone, which didn't make me nervous as it usually did because we laughed a lot. We were discovering how much we had in common, like Matt had a kid brother and I had a kid sister, almost the same age; and we both liked them, a lot. (I didn't tell Matt that sometimes Lisa annoyed me.) Matt's mother sounded a little like mine except, as Matt said, Rocky

River mothers are probably a lot alike. (I didn't want to ask Matt if his mother drank sometimes, by herself. That was too personal!) Our fathers both travelled a lot, and were under pressure, but that's true for probably ninety per cent of Rocky River fathers, at least the ones in business. (I didn't want to linger on this subject. I kind of got the impression that his father was about to be downsized...)

The most exciting thing was: we went hiking in the Rocky River Nature Preserve on Saturday afternoon. The first time I'd ever wanted to hike in that special place with anybody; and I met Pumpkin, Matt's golden retriever. A beautiful silky-haired, gentle dog with a russet-gold coat and limpid brown eyes who licked my hands like we were old friends.

"Pumpkin, this is my friend Ursula Riggs. Ursula, this is Pumpkin Donaghy."

I was surprised a guy could be so sentimental about a dog. But it made sense, with Matt. The more you got to know him, the more complex he was. Around school, with his buddies, he'd been kind of superficial, I'd always thought. Wisecracking, pretending to be laughing harder than their jokes merited. Typical guy behaviour in a group. But alone with me, Matt was almost totally different. He was nervous and excited and happy, and his breath steamed and I liked it that he was my height, and on the trail neither of us had to wait for the other to catch up; and when we talked, we talked, and did a lot of laughing; but when we didn't talk, we didn't, and it was easy and OK as Matt had said it was the first time. *Like we already knew each other from some time long ago.*

# thirty-ONE

Mom NoticEd my good mood, and looked at me kind of funny. Trying to think what this might mean, Ugly Girl not-grumpy-around-the-house?

"Are you back on the team, Ursula?"

I gave Mom this long slow one-hundred-eighty-degree camera track in utter silence. Then: "What team, Mom?"

"Oh, Ursula! *Bas*ketball. Are you—"

"N-O, Mom. I am not."

It was the second week of March. Girls' basketball at Rocky River was doing less poorly than people had predicted when Ugly Girl got huffy and quit, but except for shooting baskets in the gym by myself a few times a week, I was behaving as if I was allergic to the ball. And nobody was begging me to come back on to the team, either.

"Well, you've been staying after school so much lately. And you've been in a good mood, mostly." A sly look came into Mom's eyes.

I felt my face getting warm. I didn't want Mom, or anybody in this house, to know about Matt Donaghy. Yet. Because I didn't know, myself. I'd never been so close to anybody, I didn't know what this might mean. I flared up, pretending to be hurt. "Hey, Mom: you're saying I'm not in a good mood, like, one hundred per cent of the time? That's what you're saying?"

"Honey, I'm just – asking."

I stood there, hands on my hips. Ugly Girl in Rocky River sweatshirt, jeans, running shoes big as horses' hooves. I stood there incensed. "*I'm* just asking, Mom!"

There came Lisa into the kitchen, as if she'd been feeling lonely. She could tell by her big sis's tone of voice that Mom was being teased. "What're you asking Mom, Ursula?"

I said, "I'm not asking. I'm implying. That Mom doesn't think I'm in a good mood one hundred per cent of the time."

Lisa chortled. "Maybe just ninety-nine point nine per cent of the time, hey Mom?"

By this time Mom was laughing, shaking her head at us both. I liked to see her in a laughing mood, not sad and edgy, when Dad was away. I'd picked up these shrewd tactics of teasing from Dad, who could wriggle out of a tight spot like Tiger Woods out of a sand trap.

The best defence, said Dad, is an offence. When somebody's asking you questions you don't want to answer.

Still, Mom was suspicious.

One morning saying, like out of nowhere, "Ursula, I hear you on the phone a lot lately. Last night?"

I was at the refrigerator. I had my back to Mom. Fortunately she couldn't see Ugly Girl's stricken face.

I continued reaching for the unsweetened grapefruit juice and poured some into a glass, and by the time I turned so Mom could see me, my expression was Ugly-Girl-cool, unperturbed. "Is that a statement, Mom, or a question? It's kind of ambiguous."

Mom flushed. She wasn't in such a great mood this early in the morning. "I'm sure I heard you talking – and laughing – as late as midnight. If I hadn't been so sleepy myself—"

"Mom, I'm not aware my phone is tapped. Since when did you and Dad get a court order?"

Mom glowered. Lisa giggled. Here was Big Sis–on-the-edge-of-rude and it was only seven forty-two A.M.

"Ursula, I'm not eavesdropping on you. But I'm concerned when you're obviously wasting time on the phone, and when you stay up so late. It isn't like you."

Ugly Girl shot right back, like Ping-Pong, "Who's it like, then? Anybody I know?" My expression remained deadpan but Lisa was really giggling now.

"Ursula, don't be mouthy. I'm concerned—"

So Mom goes, frowning and peering at me with her critical Mom-eyes, the way, some other time, she might've picked at Ugly Girl because I rarely talked to anyone on the phone, never invited friends to the house, and didn't appear to be (I'd overheard her worrying on the phone, with Grandma) "socialising" with my classmates at Rocky River. (Which meant: "wasn't dating". Sure.) But now that I had a friend, and just possibly this individual was a special friend, Mom had to pick at me anyway. A FIERY RED sensation was moving up my brain stem like liquid mercury.

I spooned plain nonfat yogurt into a bowl, sprinkled it with wheat germ, added some fruit, made two pieces of eleven-grain toast, and took my grapefruit juice and departed the kitchen to eat breakfast in our solarium at the rear of the house. I knew Mom would follow, but only partway. "Ursula, I'm only thinking of *you*. How many hours' sleep did you get last night? It's been all this past week—"

"Mom, where's Dad?"

"What? Why do you – why are you asking that?"

"Is Dad on this continent, or is he in – Australia? Thailand? Germany? Where?"

"You know very well your father happens to be in Frankfurt until Friday."

"Mom, worry about Dad, OK?"

The look on Mom's face! Ugly Girl had not meant, maybe, to provoke such a reaction. Like accidentally-on-purpose colliding with an opponent on the basketball court, and knocking the wind right out of her, practically breaking a rib, and you can't mumble you're sorry because that might imply it wasn't an accident.

Mom just turned and walked back to the kitchen and left me, and I appreciated the quiet, staring into our snowy-leafy backyard, but my breakfast didn't taste so good, and breakfast was Ugly Girl's favourite meal.

FIERY RED. I was at my locker hanging up my jacket, running my fingers through my springy hair, wondering if I'd have time to talk to Matt before the last homeroom bell rang, decided no, not worth rushing into the room and looking less-than-Ursula-cool. I was wearing khakis, and a man's white cotton long-sleeved shirt, and a suede vest, and a dozen studs flashing in my ears. I was feeling good. I'd run two miles to school in the fresh cold air to clear my head of that conversation with Mom. *I hate her! She hates me!* More calmly thinking, *She feels threatened. By Matt. And Dad. What if there's another woman? Men like Dad do it all the time. Mom would break into pieces. Where would that leave Ugly Girl?* It wasn't fair, when I had my new friend Matt Donaghy and wanted to spend all my time with him.

(Did I? All my time? What did that mean?)

We'd meet for lunch as usual. The "misfits" table, which we'd transformed into a really fun, "intellectually stimulating" table. And after school we'd do homework in the library. And after that... But what is happening to Ugly Girl?

I was ransacking my locker when there came, bounding up to me, Courtney Levao flashing a big smile. "Hey Ursula."

"Hey Courtney. How's it goin'?"

It was the day after Rocky River girls' basketball had won, by fewer points than you have fingers on one hand, not counting the thumb on that hand, a hotly contested game with Bedford, another of our old, mean rivals. Anyway, that was the news I'd heard.

I told Courtney congratulations on the game. She said, "Oh. Yeah, well. We did OK, but if they'd been like Yonkers, or Tarrytown, it'd be a different, sadder story, we know that." But Courtney was smiling, she was feeling good. Probably she'd scored most of Rocky River's points the day before.

Courtney was a senior, almost as tall as Ugly Girl but lacking Ugly Girl's upper body strength and shrewd, lateral movements in the game. She could score, though, like a guy almost: gliding up to the net, sort of leaping, and seeming to drop the ball in. My most reliable starting-out forward, after myself.

We'd always gotten along. Except that last game. Courtney was one of the players who'd glared at me as if, personally, she'd have liked to rip my throat out with her teeth.

Ugly Girl never forgets.

Ugly Girl never lets down her guard.

I wasn't feeling so ugly this morning, though. Too much cramming my head.

Courtney chatted for a while about the game, then said, in an undertone, so kids on either side of my locker and milling around in the noisy corridor couldn't hear, "Schultz is saying things like, she misses you, Ursula."

I felt my face burn. I didn't let on.

"Oh come on, Courtney. That's BS Schultz hates my guts. I don't even blame her."

"Ursula, that isn't so! We all know you really were hurt, that game. I'd have gone to the ER."

This was a really weird, really agitating conversation to be having, so much confusion in the corridor, and the first bell ringing, and Courtney Levao practically in my face looking wistful. I said, "Hey, you guys are OK without me. You never got a chance, with me hogging the ball. This is your opportunity to have a great time."

"Oh, sure! A great time losing." Courtney laughed, like a kid who's been given her birthday present, opens it, and discovers some wadded tissue. "We have just three more games, Ursula. Almost, we could still make the play-offs."

Was that so? It didn't seem possible.

By the door to Mrs Carlisle's room, Matt was waiting. I always liked to see how tall he was, and that faded-red hair he'd been letting grow a little long, and how he'd be looking around, I guess, for *me*. Ugly Girl!

Courtney was saying some other things, earnest but keeping it light. I remembered now that Ms Schultz had asked Courtney to be captain when I quit, and a good team captain has one primary thing on her mind: winning. That's spelled W-I-N-N-I-N-G. I could admire that, and I had to concede that Courtney seemed genuinely friendly.

I saw Matt, and Matt saw me. He waved. He grinned. He had something to tell me that wouldn't wait till lunch, and I had some things to tell him, too. We'd been e-mailing till two A.M. that morning and it'd been a long break, 6.5 hours out of contact.

"Courtney, hey – I gotta run. I'm late. Say hi to Schultz and the girls for me, OK?"

And Ugly Girl rushed away.

FIERY RED. Dad came home from Germany and brought me back a French-language art magazine, featuring "The New Generation of European Women Artists". Mom had had her hair done, what's called highlighting, grey streaks transformed by the magic of chemistry into pale-gold streaks, and was looking pretty for a woman her age, and behaved like she'd forgiven (again) her older daughter Ursula. You could see the relief in her face, at times like these. Dad was home. Clayton Riggs had returned another time to us. I said, "Dad, why'd we never get a dog?" (This was no new query. Lisa and I had nagged Dad most of our lives for a dog, and now I'd met Matt's Pumpkin and fallen in love with her.)

Dad said, simple as you'd explain to a two-year-old, "Because we'd have to get a puppy. They start out as puppies, honey."

If I asked more questions, Dad would say, with that look of his of absolute innocence, "You know I would love a dog, Ursula. I'm an animal lover. Unfortunately I'm allergic to dog hairs. You wouldn't want me to be allergic to *home* – would you?"

FIERY RED. Those Mom-eyes! Next she's in my room, just walks in while I'm typing a message to Matt, it's after supper and Lisa and I did dishes, it's quiet-homework-time at least in theory, except Mom has been on the phone (I never listen to her friends' names, there are too many of them) and her news is – "Ursula? You and that Donaghy boy are – friends?"

My face tightens up. Like a fist. Sure, I knew that Mom would find out. It was just a question of when.

"Mom, I've got friends. I'm not, like, a total freak."

"But, Ursula – that boy? Matthew Donaghy? The one who caused all that trouble back in January? And now his parents are suing everyone in sight!"

Mom is smiling this weird dazed smile. It's a total shock, the earth caving in, is this something she's supposed to know, is it some kind of game, she's been betrayed? "Ursula, you told your father and me you didn't know the Donaghy boy."

Calmly I say, "Mom, I didn't know Matt *then*. I know him *now*."

"Well – why? Why *him*?"

FIERY RED rising in my brain. Danger!

"Alison told me her daughter says – you and Matthew Donaghy are *a couple*. At the high school. And you've never said a *word*."

The way Mom utters "a couple", it's like she has been forced to utter the name of a really loathsome, disgusting disease she'd never believed would show up in *her home*.

I want to laugh. Possibly this hysterical woman hasn't noticed, but Ugly Girl has not confided in her for years.

"Mom, you've been after me since practically fourth grade to socialise at school more. Meaning 'boys' – right? So now I have a friend who's a boy, not a boyfriend but a friend-who's-a-boy, and you're looking like I'm pregnant *and* I have AIDS. This is me, Ursula, remember?"

All Mom seems to be hearing is "pregnant *and* AIDS". She's just staring at me, breathing through her mouth like an out-of-condition athlete. "Ursula, what – are you saying? Are you being ironic, or—"

"Mom, I can't figure you. You never had time to show up for my basketball games, but you want me back on the team. You have time for Lisa but not me: OK. I can live with that. If I happened to be you, I'd be more interested in Lisa than in Ursula. But I'd also know that Ursula is sixteen years old and can make her own decisions about friends without any need for maternal hysteria." I start making motions with my computer, like to signal Mom to L-E-A-V-E because I have

W-O-R-K to do. But Mom's a warrior-woman herself, stubborn and capable of low blows.

"These Donaghys! Alison was telling me they're terribly grasping, vulgar, opportunistic people. The boy's mother – I don't know her name – is always joining committees, trying to wedge herself into our social circle. The father—"

"Mom, I'm not friends with Matt's parents. I've never even met them."

"They've tipped their hand, suing the school district. And Mr Parrish, and Mrs Hale. Who do you think will be paying them these millions of dollars? Taxpayers! *Us.* I wouldn't be surprised the entire thing was a publicity stunt, a ruse—"

All this anger! My well-bred, well-educated mother. I was a little shocked... Mom was sounding like kids at Rocky River. Kids smart enough to know better. Saying nasty things about Matt Donaghy because, now, his parents are suing the district for saying nasty things about Matt Donaghy. At school Ugly Girl keeps her cool, doesn't offer an opinion. I'm saying, almost pleading, "Mom, look. I thought you and Dad were proud of me, coming forward to help Matt back in January? You *said.*"

"Well, yes. We were...."

"I thought you were proud, getting that big-deal letter from Mr Parrish."

"Ursula, we are proud! Good conduct reports haven't exactly been your strong point since kindergarten. But now Mr Parrish is a defendant in this ugly suit, and if you're involved with the Donaghys..."

I lifted both hands in Dad's gesture. Total baffled innocence.

"Mom, please. I don't have a thing to do with that lawsuit."

"You'll be testifying for the Donaghys, don't worry. They'll drag you in. And Eveann. Anyone their lawyer can subpoena to testify. To get those fifty million dollars."

Is this so? Matt hasn't told me.

Mom says, "To what extent do you 'see' Matthew Donaghy?" She's staring at me like she's been told I have two heads and she's trying to figure out where both heads are.

I was getting angry now. This was turning into one of those situations where, in basketball, field hockey, even volleyball, Ugly Girl is going to use her size and weight to advantage in about five seconds and somebody's going down. Accidentally-on-purpose.

Wanting to say, *Friends last longer than couples. At Rocky River High, a lot longer.*

Wanting to say, *Friends last longer than marriages, sometimes. Look around you, Mom. Start counting.*

"This past weekend you went hiking twice. Were you with – him?"

I shrugged. I could feel my lower lip bulging out like – who?

That mean Brewer girl.

"Those evenings you've been at the mall – and stayed to see a movie – you said you were going with your friends, and I assumed—"

"Is this the third degree, Mom? What? I'm sixteen years old, Mom. Girls at Rocky River have been on the pill since age thirteen, and some of them are daughters of your friends."

Mom is looking stricken now. "Well. I know. But your father and I don't approve of—"

"So be grateful, Mom. Big Ursula – which is one of the kinder things the kids call me, behind my back – is a V-I-R-G-I-N and will be a V-I-R-G-I-N for a long time."

Why am I saying such things? Do I mean them?

Matt has told me this happens to him sometimes. His mouth says things he himself doesn't mean...

"You've been at the mall in those circumstances several times, Ursula. Were you with that boy all those hours?"

"Sure, Mom. We were conspiring to blow up the mall."

"Ursula!"

"Conspiring to bomb Saks and Lord & Taylor, just to inconvenience *you*."

Mom's laser eyes flash on to my computer screen. From a distance of twelve feet, maybe she can read the message I've begun to Matt. "Ursula, are you writing to him *now*? That's what you do, isn't it, you two e-mail each other, and you're on the phone all night, and—"

Mom starts forward and, defiantly, I click my e-mail off the screen.

I'm on my feet, practically clenching my fists.

"Leave me alone, Mom. *Je ne suis pas vous.* I am not you."

Fast and furious as the closing seconds of a basketball game in which, if you aren't careful, you can get seriously injured.

"Your father will have an opinion on this, young lady."

Young lady! Mom is totally crazed.

Mom turns and walks out and slams my door behind her and I'm crouched there trembling, heart pounding and chill sweat all over my body.

And the phone rings.

"Ursula? It's me."

"Matt!"

"You sound sort of – breathless? Is something wrong?"

"I – no. Nothing is wrong."

"I was wondering why you hadn't answered my two e-mails since school, so I thought I'd call. Is that OK? Or – are you working?"

"It's OK, Matt. I was just going to call *you*."

# thirty-two

**at Rocky River** High, through the month of March, everybody had an opinion of the new friends.

"Can you believe it! Those two."

They were seen walking together in the corridors. They were seen in the cafeteria at noon. They were seen in the library after school, studying together. They were reported seen hiking together in the Rocky River Nature Preserve and at Croton State Park, on a steep trail that led down to the Hudson River. Hiking, they were accompanied by a golden retriever.

"It's his. Matt's. Pumpkin. He's had her for ever."

They were seen at the Cinemax at the Rocky River Mall, and at Starbucks at the mall, and at Tower Records; they were seen shopping together at the Gap and Clothes Barn. They were seen at Santa Fe Express, at the Orchid Pavilion, at the Whole Earth Art Gallery and Café. The Gypsy Horse Art Gallery & Café. Barnes & Noble. Sakura House. Potters'

Village. Brooke Tyler, who'd gone into Manhattan with visiting relatives, claimed she'd seen them at the Metropolitan Museum of Art – "Sitting in the courtyard of the American wing. On a bench. Like an actual *couple.*" Denis Wheeler, whose uncle was an off-Broadway theatrical producer, claimed he'd seen them at a play performance – "A really weird comedy by some playwright named Nicky Silver. Just the kind of far-out humour Matt Donaghy would go for."

Opinion was about equally divided on whether Ursula Riggs and Matt Donaghy were just friends or more than just friends. Even those who reported on them most avidly couldn't claim that they'd seen them "holding hands, ever. Or even making out, a little."

"They're just friends, obviously. No normal guy would be attracted to Big Ursula."

"Are you kidding? Ursula's terrific. Matt's the creep. Why'd she be attracted to *him*?"

"Well, they're both misfits. Obviously."

Stacey Flynn said, "Matt is in a state of shock. Since those detectives took him out of Mr Weinberg's study hall, he hasn't been himself. Going out with Ursula Riggs is, like, a symptom of his nervous breakdown." Stacey felt very sorry for Matt and for his parents, but it was too awkward for her to talk to him right now – she hoped he would understand.

The senior jocks who talked openly of how they'd like to "show Donaghy what happens to traitors" were disgusted by the very idea of Matt Donaghy and Ursula Riggs. "He's a fag. She's a bull dyke. Go figure."

Mr Weinberg, asked his opinion of Rocky River's newest and most controversial couple, declined to give it – "None of your business, kids."

Gordon Kim, now vice president of the junior class, shook his head and laughed over all the fuss. "Donaghy, Riggs – they're both *tall*, that's why. It's logical."

# thirty-three

**HE asked me,** so I told him.

If he didn't want me to tell him, why'd he ask?

Sure, I might've guessed it was a mistake. But I was thinking he had such high regard for me. *Ursula Riggs. 1 individual in 1 million. Like we already knew each other from some time long ago.*

It was like climbing those steps to the high board and knowing you're not going to climb back down. You're going to dive.

"Matt, I think it's a mistake."

Not what Matt wanted to hear from his friend Ursula, I guess.

"You asked me, so that's my opinion. I'm sorry."

"OK, Ursula. Thanks. I appreciate your honesty."

But that was all he said. He began walking faster. And we'd been walking pretty fast already. Up a fairly steep hill. Pumpkin was trotting beside us, breath steaming. It was getting hard for her, a thick-bodied dog her age, to keep up with us. She had to pretend she was interested in sniffing out something, pausing for a few seconds to catch her breath, maybe stopping for a quick inspired pee on a log, before trotting after us.

Matt was so distracted, he'd have forgotten poor Pumpkin completely. I was the one to encourage her – "Pum'kin! *Good* dog. C'mon."

It was a fierce-bright-cold morning. We were hiking on a trail above the Hudson River, in Croton State Park; we'd been hiking here lately, driving in Matt's car, so that nobody from Rocky River was likely to see us.

"Matt, hey? You asked me. So I told you."

"OK, Ursula. I *said*."

He was angry with me. Matt Donaghy was angry with me!

The first time ever. I was feeling so hurt.

"Matt, you've been asking me and I told you it's none of my business, I don't judge, and that's true, I don't judge *you*. But if you ask me what I think of the lawsuit, meaning your parents' judgement..."

Matt just kept walking up the trail. His face was turned from me – I saw just his profile looking shut up, sullen. He'd jammed his wool cap down on to his forehead. His faded-red hair was looking a little snarled. Pumpkin and I trotted to keep up with his long strides.

Well, he'd asked. So I'd told him.

The lawsuit. The damned lawsuit that was all Matt's parents talked about now. ("It's like a fire roaring out of control inside a forest," Matt told me, "except the fire is in our house. It's the Donaghys' *life*.")

You'd never realise what a big deal a lawsuit is. If you're involved personally. It just doesn't go away. Everybody knew what the Donaghys were demanding: $50 million. They were suing Parrish, Hale, some Rocky River School District officials including the superintendent, and they were suing Reverend Brewer, on charges of "malicious slander", "defamation of character", "professional malpractice...". There was a lot more to it that I didn't want to know. Now that the lawyers on both sides were into it, and so-called developments were leaked to the media, it was getting complicated like some disease that breaks down one organ, then another, then another.

"Matt, hey. I know you and your parents went through a lot, and you're angry, but—"

"You don't know, Ursula. Not really."

These words Matt sort of tossed over his shoulder, not looking at me.

I felt my face getting warm, even on the trail above the river.

This was so unfair. He'd asked me my opinion, he must've known what I might say.

(Or, maybe: I'd been thinking Matt would naturally agree with me. He was disgusted, too, with the lawsuit – wasn't he?)

Ugly Girl was nudging in here. Ugly Girl liked a good fight she was morally certain she should win.

"Matt, you'd asked me weeks ago what I thought about the lawsuit. You said *please* to tell you the truth! Don't think I haven't been feeling bad about it too. I can see what it's doing to you, and that's why—"

"You don't know what it's doing to me, Ursula. And you don't know what it's doing to my parents."

This was shocking, it was so unfair. It was inaccurate too: in his e-mails and on the phone and in conversations Matt had told me how the lawsuit was "tearing me up" – "making people hate me all the more" – "driving my dad and mom totally crazy". When Matt said these things, I listened sympathetically because I didn't judge him, but I'd always had my own thoughts about the lawsuit. I'd only just kept quiet about them.

Maybe I should've kept quiet now. But Ugly Girl was feeling betrayed, tricked.

"The lawsuit just seems wrong to me. It just seems – well, like making things worse. It's nothing I would want to do, maybe that's all I'm saying. Matt? See? I'm a hothead too. But then I figure, these things backfire."

Matt shrugged. I couldn't believe this: he was furious with me for telling the truth. And he'd asked me to tell him this truth!

I said, "People get the wrong idea, a lawsuit like this is being done for just – well, money. And so much money."

Now Matt did turn to me, and I saw that his eyes were brimming with tears, and his mouth was trembling.

I couldn't believe the shocking thing Matt said to me, in a voice bitter and heavy with sarcasm – "My dad isn't rich like yours, Ursula. Maybe the Donaghys *need money*."

And he practically trotted up the trail, like he couldn't bear to be anywhere close to me. I considered turning around and going back down, waiting for him at the car, better yet getting a ride back to Rocky River somehow else, leaving *him*, but there was Pumpkin panting and looking clearly unhappy, aware of tension between Matt and me, so Pumpkin and I kept a slower pace, behind Matt, and I wondered if Matt was crying, if a boy could cry, out of hurt but also out of anger, the way girls do, though not Ugly Girl. I wiped at my eyes, annoyed that they were wet, it must've been caused by the March wind off the river for Ugly Girl doesn't cry.

# thirty-four

NO E-mails awaiting me in the morning, posted by *Your friend Matt* during the night. No telephone calls. If Mom was listening, she must've been pleased. At school we sat at the same table for lunch, the misfits' table, talking and even laughing (pretty convincingly, I thought) with the others. It was like a really painful game in which, though you're losing, you have to keep playing your best because people are watching and expect a certain standard of performance from you.

I didn't cry. I would not cry.

I would not give in, either.

# thirty-five

**Matt WaSN't goiNg** to give in.

Feeling like a time bomb. A secret bomb, and nobody knows when it will explode because the clock's hands have been broken off. Tick-tick-ticking inside. But you wouldn't want to hold it against your ear, to hear that ticking.

He'd lost her now. Ursula. Matt's only friend.

Still, he would not give in.

He missed her. He missed their e-mail correspondence. Now he had no one. He missed calling her at midnight as he'd been doing, their digital watches so synchronised that Ursula lifted the receiver of her phone in the first nanosecond of the first ring.

"Hi! It's me."

"Hi."

They'd only been friends for a few weeks, but.

They'd never held hands or kissed or... but.

At school Matt wanted to shield his eyes from her. She was so tall, walked with such pride. He saw her blue eyes glance upon him with contempt. She was a person of integrity, he was a coward.

She had no right to criticise his parents! *People get the wrong idea, a lawsuit like this is being done for just money.*

He hated her.

# thirty-six

"**Matt, where are** you? It's time."

It was Matt's mother calling him. Trying to make her voice bright, bubbly, "optimistic".

They were going to see Dr Harpie. The "renowned" Dr Harpie, whose office was at Park Avenue and 72nd Street, Manhattan. In Dr Harpie's best-selling *Adolescents at Risk: Your Child and Depression* it was stated: "Young depressives often take their cues from elder family depressants," so it was important to shield an impressionable young person from adult depression, anxiety, and above all, "suicidal attitudes".

Matt's mother hadn't liked the happy face he'd drawn in Dr Harpie's book. "Is this your idea of a joke, Matt?" she'd asked him with a hurt smile. "If so, it isn't funny. Under the circumstances."

An apology was expected. Matt laughed instead.

•   •   •

"Pumpkin. *You* can't come with us, you're too normal. No 'suicidal attitudes'."

Before leaving, Matt checked his computer. No mail.

It was humiliating. Matt's mother insisted upon driving him into the city. "You don't trust me to go alone, right?" Matt asked, and his mom said quickly, "Of course I trust you, Matt. But I'm expected to speak with Dr Harpie too."

*But you don't know me. Not the first thing.*

No one except Ursula Riggs knew. That day in the preserve, by Rocky River Creek.

Matt had agreed to see Dr Harpie only because both his parents had put pressure on him. They claimed to be "very concerned" about him, and probably this was so, yet at the same time Matt guessed that seeing a psychiatrist was part of their legal strategy. Mr Leacock had advised them. In the Donaghys' lawsuit it would be impressive that Matthew had suffered such psychological distress that he was seeing a psychiatrist. A renowned specialist in troubled adolescents who has agreed to speak to the court.

Matt was sullen and uncommunicative – "uncommunicative" was a term frequently used in Dr Harpie's book – on the drive into the city. He'd wanted to drive, of course, but his mom insisted she would drive, she "didn't trust" his mood. Matt said sarcastically, "Meaning what, Mom? You think I might drive us into the Hudson River? Matricide-suicide?" Matt's mother winced. She'd applied crimson lipstick to her mouth, but the skin around her mouth was white. "Jokes like that are not funny, Matt. You know better."

Sure I do. I know a lot better. But Big Mouth doesn't give a damn.

When they entered Dr Harpie's office, Matt suddenly balked and refused to stay. He told his astonished mother that he was leaving – "I'm out of here, Mom. This isn't for me." Matt's mother seized his wrist with surprisingly strong fingers. "Matt, you are not leaving. You are not walking out of here, *you have an appointment.*"

"It's your appointment, Mom. *You* see him."

Matt took a deep breath. He had to say this, no matter how angry his father would be. "Dad, I'm sorry. I've changed my mind. I don't want you to sue."

Matt's father stared at him. "Certainly we're going to sue, Matt. It's too late to change your mind. You've been slandered – libelled. *We* have been. It's pointless even to discuss this."

"But we need to discuss it, Dad. Please."

"Matt, the lawsuit is under way. Motions have been filed. A court date has been named: April twenty-seventh. That's coming up soon. Leacock doesn't come cheaply, you know." Matt's father laughed, but it was a grim laugh.

"I can't go through with it. Giving more testimony, answering more questions... I want to forget it."

"Forget it? Never. *We* aren't going to forget it."

"People are saying... the lawsuit only makes things worse. Some of them have the wrong idea we're doing it for just – money."

"So, what's wrong with money?" Matt's father laughed again, and his laughter turned into coughing. His face, which had once been a handsome, fair-skinned face, with wide-set grey-green eyes like Matt's, was now florid and slack. Mr Donaghy had been away for several days and appeared not to have shaved for part of that time. Matt no longer knew if his father had an actual job or was already in a "transitional" state, and he couldn't ask his mother, who refused to answer such questions. Alex had asked Matt the other evening, "Does Dad have a job now? Where does he *go*?" Matt felt sorry for his kid brother, who was beginning to share some of the anxieties of the household. "Leacock expects us to win in court. Any reasonably intelligent judge, hearing how the school district treated you, will find for us. Or the district may offer us a generous settlement. Either way we'll be publicly vindicated."

"Dad, people around here are all hating us. At school—"

"Ignore them. They're your enemies. We'll transfer you to a first-rate private school, starting next fall."

Matt knew that his parents were discussing a boarding school in Massachusetts. An expensive school especially geared for very bright adolescents with "problems of social adjustment".

Matt's father continued, in a rapid, vehement voice, "Look what those people tried to do to you, Matt. Mr Parrish – who should have protected you – handed you over to the police like a common criminal. The detectives were pressing you to confess. They wanted you to name co-conspirators. You said so yourself. What if you'd broken down, given in? It was like a witch hunt. Without a shred of evidence, only the false, lying testimony of right-wing religious fanatics with a history of causing trouble in this community, they've destroyed our reputation." Matt's father paused, breathing quickly. "And we want our revenge."

Matt said, miserably, "But Dad, I don't want revenge. I just want..."

What? Things to be the way they'd been, before the arrest?

But Matt wouldn't have gotten to know Ursula Riggs in that case. He'd still have his old hypocrite friends.

Matt's father began to shout at him. "It doesn't matter what you want, Matt. We're in this too far to back out. My name is at stake – my integrity. Just remember, you got us into this – with your idiotic, childish sense of humour."

# thirty-SEVEN

*Ugly Girl, NO* tears. *And no looking back.*
   *Never, never give in.*

Mom looked at me in this searching, almost-sympathetic way.
Wanting to ask, maybe, why I wasn't any longer talking and
laughing on the phone later than she approved of, and why I
was so quiet, a big horsy sullen girl with a pouty lower lip
who'd been, until just recently, in a Good Mood.

Wanting to ask what had happened between me and Matt
Donaghy.

"Ursula? There's nothing wrong, is there?"

"Absolutely not, Mom. What about you?"

I was getting mean again, the way I'd been before getting
to know Matt, and before quitting the team. Scoring a point,
scoring a wisecrack, scoring a blow like an elbow in the rib, an
accidentally-on-purpose foul.

Except with Lisa. I guess I loved Lisa. I'd overhear her talking with her ballet-class friends, these sweet little girls with such slender sparrow bodies, chests still flat, feet half the size of Ugly Girl's. I'd want to hug Lisa and protect her. Not just from the dancing lessons and recitals and so much pressure on a girl so young, but from something else, headed for her, that I couldn't name.

She won't be protected like Ugly Girl.

But I was thinking, maybe I'd been wrong to speak to Matt as I had? Criticising his parents. Sure, you can criticise your own parents, but you don't want anyone else to criticise them.

Three days had passed since our hike in Croton Park. When we'd driven back to Rocky River scarcely saying a word. *He doesn't like me. Well, I hate him!* When Matt let me out, I hugged Pumpkin in a fierce, hard embrace. "Goodbye, Pum'kin! Be good." Like it really was goodbye, I'd never see her again.

Three days. I wasn't eating much, I guess. I could tell I'd lost weight – my clothes were loose.

So I logged on to my e-mail (where there was a message, but from Bonnie, and it wasn't important) and typed this out, for Matt.

Tues 3/20/01  11:43 PM

20 mars
dear matt--
i'm sorry. i miss you.

u r

This pathetic little message required ten minutes to compose; then instead of clicking SEND I lost my nerve and clicked DELETE.

Easier that way.

# thirty-eight

"Ursula, what's that? 'Treasure hunt'?"

Was it a joke? A trick? My hand turned the stiff piece of paper, which had been stuck into the crack of my locker door at school. Eveann and I stared at it, mystified. It was about the size of a dollar bill, black construction paper with sparkling gold lettering:

TREASURE HUNT COUPON. FOR U R ONLY.
Go to Library.
Turn left.
Below farthest-left window,
2nd shelf.

At Rocky River High there was an atmosphere of tension. It had to do with the Donaghys' lawsuit, and people taking sides, and Matt continuing to attend classes, stubborn, and seemingly indifferent to hostility, but it also had to do with an interview Reverend Brewer had given in a local paper, charging Rocky River school authorities with hiring "morally unfit teachers" (Brewer didn't name any names, but it was obvious he was referring to Mr Steiner) and "coddling teenaged terrorists" (still campaigning against Matt). It was a long, rambling interview, allegedly about the injustice of Reverend Brewer being sued, and having to start a legal defence fund among his congregation and in the community, since the Rocky River School District was declining to pay his legal expenses. And his daughters Muriel and Miriam, who'd only "done their duty as Christian U.S. citizens," were subject to sarcasm and hostility from classmates and teachers both, and in danger of not graduating with their class.

You could try to ignore Reverend Brewer, but there he was: in your face.

Brewer had the moon face of his twin daughters, but he was tough-looking as a Marine sergeant, with creased skin, a few strands of wirelike hair on his head, and an angry squint like somebody staring into the sun. He'd moved to Westchester County twenty-two years ago, he said, to establish the Apostles of Jesus in a mission "in the very heart of the Antichrist", out of private funds.

Antichrist? Did that mean Jews? Or – anybody Reverend Brewer took a dislike to?

So, finding this "coupon" in my locker, I halfway thought it might have something to do with Brewer. Muriel and Miriam avoided me, as I avoided them, but playing weird tricks was exactly the kind of thing they might do.

Still, I was too curious about the "treasure hunt coupon" not to follow instructions. I went to the library; turned left, back below the farthest-left window there were bookshelves for oversized books, atlases of the world, and slipped in among them was a book in a wrapper lettered in the same sparkly gold.

## IF U ARE UR THIS IS FOR U

I laughed. This was like a kids' game!

I pulled off the wrapping paper, and the book was *Great Twentieth Century Drawings*. It was a book I'd been browsing in when Matt and I went to the Metropolitan Museum of Art one Sunday afternoon and spent time in the bookstore.

Tears stung my eyes. Matt had bought this for me!

Inside the front cover was his note:

> Just because he has a Big Mouth
> Just because he is Uncouth Youth
> Does not mean he can't speak Truth.
>
> Dear Ursula,
> I'm sorry.
> You were right, & I was wrong.
> I miss you.
>
> Your friend Matt

I grabbed the book and ran from the library, and located Matt (whose schedule I'd memorised) just headed downstairs for history class. I was so excited, I grabbed his arm, and his hand closed over mine. "Oh Matt – thanks!" We were sort of stumbling on the stairs, bumping into people. I was almost crying, or maybe was crying, and Matt was just grinning at me. "I hope you like it, Ursula." I said thanks again, and Matt was holding my hand in his like he didn't want to let it go, and people were annoyed because we were blocking the traffic flow on the stairs, but some of them were looking amused, like they knew all about us, and this just confirmed their suspicions. I felt my face burn, so exposed. I laughed, and backed away. "See you after school, Matt?"

Matt called after me, "I'll be there."


We went to the Gypsy Horse Café. And afterwards, for two hours we just walked.

Matt told me about quarrelling with his father, how he hated the lawsuit himself, he'd always hated it, and he was contemplating just refusing to cooperate any longer with their lawyer, and refusing to testify in court on April 27 – "And maybe that will end it."

I said, "You'd still have to live with your father, Matt. It might not be so easy."

We got to talking about our fathers. I found myself telling him how I'd overheard Dad talking about my size, how I'd been hurt. "Because he was right. Dad always is right."

But Matt was shaking his head. He didn't agree.

"You're beautiful, Ursula. Not like other girls but – in your own way. Special."

I was blushing, with a fierce painful heat.

Beautiful? Ugly Girl?

"Don't make a face, Ursula. I'm serious."

"I'm not making a face, this *is* my face."

I laughed, but Matt didn't join me. He knew what I was doing, making nervous fun of myself. But he wouldn't join in.

"Around school, the way you carry yourself, you look like – well, some Olympic athlete. You have a terrific smile, and a sense of humour almost as weird as mine." Matt was talking slowly, almost stumblingly, with an uncertain smile, not knowing what he was saying. My heart was beating so quickly, I could scarcely breathe. "People are afraid of you because you can be sarcastic, but they respect you, for sure." Matt touched my shoulder, and my hair, the first time he'd ever touched me like that, and a sensation of warmth spread through me, but I was afraid, and in danger of bursting into high-pitched giggles, and stepped away. *I can pretend that didn't happen. Maybe it was an accident?*

"Ursula? What are you laughing at?"

"I'm not laughing! I'm shivering, I guess."

It was windy, at dusk of a March day when the sky was the hue and texture of old, gritty, soiled snow.

We were walking up into the hilly neighbourhoods behind Rocky River Boulevard, where I lived. Evidently Matt was walking me home in a circuitous way.

He told me about his mother driving him into the city, to the fancy shrink's office on Park Avenue, and how he'd walked out, and since then she was "supremely disgusted" with him, where before she'd been "only normally disgusted". I asked him what his mother thought about the lawsuit, did she agree with his father, and Matt made a flapping motion with his arms, like a penguin, and said, "Mom is *disgusted* with me. No further comment."

I tried to think: was my mom disgusted with me at the moment?

I began to laugh, and Matt asked, "What?" and I said, "I don't know, it's just funny. People are disgusted with you, and people are disgusted with me. So – here we are."

Matt said, "It's only logical."

We laughed harder. Tears ran down our cheeks. It *was* hilarious – wasn't it?

# thirty-NINE

**TWO Nights later,** the phone rang and I answered it and it was Matt. "You won't believe what's happened, Ursula. What they've done to us now."

It was so: I could hardly believe it.

That night, Ugly Girl did cry. In rage, and pity.

# forty

 alex ran home crying.

"Pumpkin is gone, Mom! They took Pumpkin!"

It was six twenty P.M. Friday. Alex had been walking the golden retriever in the hilly residential neighbourhood in which the Donaghys lived, where houses were set on wooded lots of about two acres and properties were set off from one another by six-foot fences. The drives and lanes of suburban Rocky River curved, and though there were sidewalks, few residents walked. There were few cars passing. It was dusk; wet snowflakes were lightly falling. Alex would tell his mother tearfully that he'd unsnapped Pumpkin's leash as he usually did, letting her loose, since she was so well trained and never trotted far away. Five minutes later, Pumpkin was gone.

Matt hadn't come home from school directly. He'd gone with Ursula to the Rocky River Public Library, where they researched their history projects, and afterwards they'd been in Starbucks for another hour. It was the happiest time Matt had had in memory: talking with Ursula, relaxed and laughing. Ursula was encouraging Matt to rejoin the Drama Club, and to write a new play, a comedy – "about how misfits get along. Once they decide, what the hell, they're *misfits*." Matt was encouraging Ursula to rejoin the basketball team before it was too late. "It seems like, from what you say, it's just your pride stopping you," Matt said. Ursula laughed. "'Just my pride'? That's me." By the time Matt arrived at his home, Pumpkin had been missing for a half hour.

Matt entered the kitchen, and Alex ran to him. "They took Pumpkin, Matt!" The boy's face was wet with tears and his voice trembled. "A car came by, they stopped, and I heard Pumpkin barking, and a door slam, and – she was gone."

Matt asked, astonished, "Who took Pumpkin?"

Alex cried, "I don't know, Matt! I'm sorry! I wasn't watching, I guess. I mean – I didn't know anybody would take her, why would anybody take Pumpkin? I think they must've passed by me, in an SUV, and circled the block and came up behind me again, and Pumpkin was sniffing around at the top of the hill by that big brick house with the columns, and – they took her."

Alex hadn't been able to see who was in the SUV but he was pretty certain there were at least two people.

It was like something on TV, Alex said. It happened so *fast*.

Matt knew what this was. "They've kidnapped Pumpkin, to punish me."

"To punish us," Matt's mother said.

Matt's mother telephoned the police. She tried to speak calmly, repeating what Alex had told her, but her voice shook and she began to cry. Matt took the receiver from her. He said, "Somebody took our dog. Yes, it was deliberate. No, she didn't 'run off'. I said *somebody took our dog,* about an hour ago. She's a golden retriever, about seven years old. Maybe seventy pounds. My brother was walking her on Arlington Circle and somebody in an SUV came by and forced her inside and drove off." Matt answered the dispatcher's perfunctory questions with rising impatience. "We've got some enemies in Rocky River, I guess."

Sure it sounded paranoid, ridiculous.

The fact that it happened to be true was no consolation.

Matt and Alex went outside to search for Pumpkin, calling her name loudly – "Pumpkin! Hey, Pumpkin!" They rang doorbells, asking their startled neighbours if they'd seen a golden retriever or an unfamiliar SUV. Though Matt knew it was futile. Pumpkin had been taken from *him*. The anxiety, hurt, anger he was feeling, worst of all the frustration, were part of it.

Alex kept saying he was sorry, it was his fault, and Matt told him no, no, it was not his fault.

"If it's anybody's fault, it's mine. But that doesn't help Pumpkin, does it?"

After forty minutes, two Rocky River patrolmen came to investigate. If they recognised the name Donaghy, they gave no indication, taking notes as Matt, Mrs Donaghy and Alex answered their questions. Alex told and retold his account of what had happened. More than once he was asked: "You didn't get a look at the licence plate, son?"

No. It was too dark to see. The SUV was too far away.

And it had happened so fast.

Matt knew that Alex was being made to feel as if he'd failed. He'd made a crucial mistake, he'd done something wrong. A ten-year-old boy! Thin faced, tearful, shivering. Matt's mother put her arms around Alex to warm him. Matt said, trying to keep the sarcasm out of his voice, "Maybe if you put out an alert? Now? Before more time passes? You could catch these people while they still have Pumpkin?" The police officers assured Matt that an alert would be sent out immediately, as soon as their reports were complete and could be filed. Pumpkin was described in detail, and the police were given several snapshots of her. "Looks like a nice dog," one commented. "Golden retrievers are good dogs. They can get spooked, though, and run off. It happens."

"It didn't just *happen*," Matt said excitedly. "It was made to happen."

Matt's mother intervened to explain that there was animosity towards the Donaghy family in Rocky River, and that the dog snatching was obviously related to it. This fact, too, the officers took down without comment. "These clippings have been sent to us in the past month," Matt's mother said, showing the officers several newspaper clippings she'd taken out of a drawer. "All from the same person, I'm sure." Matt and Alex exchanged a surprised glance: they'd known of one of these clippings, with the scrawled red ink message, but not the others.

Matt was wondering why the police officers didn't ask him about "enemies". He waited, but they did not. When they were about to leave, he said, "There've been incidents at school... guys harassing me, calling me names." He paused. He couldn't bring himself to look at his mother or Alex. He'd told no one, and now it seemed like part of his shame, that he hadn't told. And it was so demeaning! As if Matt Donaghy was a first-class wimp, telling tales to authority. But he wanted Pumpkin back – he was desperate. Pumpkin didn't deserve to be punished because of *him*. The officers asked Matt to provide names of people who'd harassed him, and Matt named the senior jocks Trevor Cassity, Duane Stanton, and one or two others... Yet for some reason he couldn't add that these guys had actually struck him, beaten him, pushed him down a flight of concrete steps and walked away laughing. Not knowing, not caring, if Matt had been seriously injured, even killed. *Fag. Sue us!* It would be their word against Matt's, wouldn't it?

"And are there others, son? Who might have taken your dog?"

Matt's face burned. Of course there were others. Too many to name without sounding ridiculous. And Pumpkin might well have been taken by someone Matt didn't know, had never seen, and could not have named. In Reverend Brewer's interview in the Rocky River weekly the angry minister had claimed he had "hundreds" of supporters in the region, he was receiving "thousands" of dollars for his defence fund.

The Rocky River patrolmen left, in no hurry. They addressed Mrs Donaghy. "We'll see what we can do about

Pumpkin, ma'am. What will probably happen is your dog will be back home by morning, good and hungry."

Matt said sarcastically, "Thanks a lot, officers!"

Matt's mother took a sleeping pill and went to bed early.

Where was Matt's father? Neither Matt nor Alex could ask.

Matt called Ursula at eleven oh three P.M. and told her the news.

"Oh Matt! Poor Pumpkin! This is terrible."

Matt's voice trembled. "I just hate them so much, Ursula. I hate them. So much."

"Matt, you don't know who they are, exactly. You can't be sure."

"The Brewers. Reverend 'Ike'. The football players. Kids who sneer at me every day in school. Who call me fag." Matt paused. Maybe Ursula didn't know this? Well, now she knew. He said, wiping at his eyes, "My mom showed the police more clippings she'd been sent, that I didn't know about. It's Brewer, or somebody in his congregation, sending that shit, I bet."

Ursula said, "Maybe it's an actual kidnapping. A dognapping. Maybe they're going to ask for a ransom."

"Or maybe just kill Pumpkin and dump her body on our lawn."

"Matt! Don't talk that way."

"Which way should I talk?" Matt asked sarcastically. "'Optimistically'?"

•   •   •

Matt and Alex meant to keep a vigil for Pumpkin through the night, downstairs in the family room.

Except by one ten A.M. Alex had fallen asleep on the sofa, exhausted, his eyes reddened from crying. Matt pulled a quilt over him. Matt vowed he would never – repeat: never – say another sarcastic, unkind, or bullying word to his brother again in his lifetime. *Never!*

Several times that night, Matt called the Rocky River police to ask if there'd been any developments. He was politely informed that, if and when there were developments, he would be called.

He wandered the darkened house. He was too restless to sit at his computer. He'd have liked to e-mail Ursula, but he guessed his mood would be too sour, too angry, it wouldn't be right to subject her to his thoughts, she might like him less, or decide she didn't like him at all. Or Matt might type out a message detailing his own hatred and how he'd like to kill, yes he'd like to bomb and shoot certain people, and a lot of them, he'd love to kill his enemies, if it would bring back Pumpkin he wouldn't hesitate for a minute... and if Matt clicked SEND, and sent such a damning message out into cyberspace where nothing is ever lost and everything can be used against you, what then?

*Big Mouth. Don't make the same mistake twice.*

He switched on the TV. But the Westchester cable channel hadn't yet posted Pumpkin on their "lost" animal site.

It was one thirty A.M., seven hours after Pumpkin's kidnapping. Matt tried to call the cable channel but got only a recorded message.

At two A.M. the phone rang, just once. By the time Matt picked up the receiver, the caller had hung up.

At three A.M. the phone rang twice. This time too Matt picked up the receiver and the caller hung up.

Matt said, begging, "Hey, c'mon! Please. She's just an innocent dog. She never hurt you, she..." Matt began to cry, wiping his nose with the edge of his hand. He was feeling weak now – his anger had subsided. The adrenaline rush had subsided. A sensation of sick horror washed over him. He thought of the sweet-natured dog who, even as a puppy, had been shy among strangers. He thought of Pumpkin's terror, her whining and whimpering, the convulsive trembling of her back legs, her cringing tail. Could Pumpkin sleep? Would they feed her?

Would they torture her?

The hairs on the back of Matt's neck stirred. He'd seen a TV film, a horror film, in which a family's dog was taken, and parts of the dog (an ear, a paw, the tail) were left on the front porch, smeared in blood.

"They wouldn't be that cruel, they couldn't be. Not to Pumpkin."

Matt couldn't recall how the TV film ended. Maybe he hadn't seen the ending. A bloodbath, probably. But who killed whom, and how, was a blank.

He didn't have a gun. His dad didn't own guns. He had no idea how you got a gun, actually. If Pumpkin wasn't returned and Matt had to take revenge, he hadn't any idea how he would do it.

Groggy from lack of sleep, Matt shut his eyes. He'd turned

the TV to mute but it seemed to him he could hear humming, buzzing. Voices. Jeering laughter. Suddenly he was seeing Trevor Cassity's face, and there was Duane Stanton, and the others. He was lying on his side in a fetal position, trying to protect his belly, his head. They were kicking him, and they were kicking Pumpkin. *So sue us! Fag! Sue us!*

But those guys weren't monsters. They were just typical Rocky River kids, Westchester kids, spoiled, used to attention because they'd been jocks since middle school, and good-looking. They weren't well liked but they were "popular".

Lots of guys envied them. Hated their guts, but envied them.

Matt wondered if the police had contacted them. Probably not.

Their word against Matthew Donaghy's word.

The fact was, anyone could have taken Pumpkin. Anyone who knew where the Donaghys lived, and was familiar with their ritual of walking the dog in the early evening, and had reason to hate them.

Most of the time Matt walked Pumpkin. Alex walked her only once or twice a week, and Mrs Donaghy less frequently. Pumpkin had always been Matt's dog. His responsibility.

If Pumpkin had been taken from *him*, what could Matt have done?

Matt was wakened by a ringing phone close beside his head.

It was six A.M. He'd fallen asleep on the sofa, the TV screen was still on, sound muted.

Matt fumbled to answer the phone – "Hello? Hel*lo*?" At

first there was no sound, then he heard it: the yipping, whining cries of a dog in pain.

"Pumpkin? *Pumpkin!*"

The line went dead.

# forty-one

"Maybe I can help somehow? At least I can be with you."

So Ursula Riggs came to Matt Donaghy's house for the first time, and was introduced to Mrs Donaghy, on the Saturday morning after Pumpkin was abducted.

Under other, normal circumstances this would have been a significant occasion for Matt and Ursula. But now Matt was so distracted by the situation, waiting always for the phone to ring, he barely had time to worry how Ursula and his mother would like each other. ("Is this Ursula Riggs your girlfriend, Matt?" Mrs Donaghy asked, puzzled, before Ursula arrived. "The girl who helped you by talking to Mr Parrish?" Stony faced, Matt just shrugged.)

By ten A.M. the Westchester cable channel was posting Pumpkin's photo above the caption HAVE YOU SEEN ME? and the brief paragraph:

PUMPKIN – 7-yr-old female golden
retriever reported abducted 3/23
Arlington Circle area Rocky River,
NY. Reward.

The Donaghys' name was not listed, but their telephone
and address were provided.

Also by ten A.M. there were no new developments
reported by Rocky River police. When Matt's mother called
headquarters, asking to speak with one of the patrolmen
who'd come to the house, she was informed that both officers
were off duty on Saturday; but of course the case was being
"pursued".

Matt took the phone receiver from his mother, intending
to ask exactly how the case was being pursued, but the
individual at the other end had already hung up.

After receiving the six-A.M. call, Matt had called Rocky
River police to report it and was told that a police officer
would be calling him back, but no one had. "My dog was being
tortured, I could hear her. I'm sure that's what it was. Can't you
help us? Please!" Matt was begging. He was on the verge of
tears. And, though it was only dawn, so tired.

Matt gauged by Ursula's startled expression that he must
look about as bad as he felt. Bruiselike circles under his eyes,
for sure. "I feel as if I've been running a marathon all night.
And I haven't gotten anywhere."

Ursula said vehemently, "We'll find Pumpkin, Matt! We
will."

It was too frustrating to wait by the phone, so Matt, Ursula and Alex went out to canvass the neighbourhood another time, in Matt's car. They drove slowly along the curving streets, seeing few people as they called "Pumpkin! Pump-kin!" out the windows of the car. It was a bright, damp morning; the sun sliced into Matt's corneas like a laser. He wasn't able to register the strangeness of Ursula beside him in the passenger seat and Alex in the backseat, his closest friend and his kid brother riding in his car on a Saturday morning, the three of them as focused upon their mission as survivors in a small life raft.

Matt drove aimlessly. Out to Main Street, where traffic was heavier, and along Route 9. Here there were pedestrians on the sidewalks, and occasionally dogs on leashes. "Look!" – Alex kept saying, nervously, each time he saw a dog whose shape, size and colouring remotely resembled Pumpkin's. Matt drove along the edge of the Rocky River Nature Preserve thinking maybe – oh, just maybe – Pumpkin's abductors might have left her out here. He drove into the suburb of Tarrytown, and north to Ossining, and back south through Rocky River to Briarcliff Manor and beyond. "I guess we're just wasting time," he said miserably. "I don't know what else to do."

Ursula had to admit she didn't know either.

They returned to the Donaghys' house. Nothing seemed to have changed. Matt's mother was sitting listlessly, drinking coffee, in the family room off the kitchen, staring at the cable channel on the screen. Matt was embarrassed to see that she still wore her bathrobe, knotted tightly at her waist. Her dark hair was dishevelled, threaded with grey delicate as cobwebs. Why couldn't she have changed into daytime clothes, combed her hair and put on lipstick? Matt was especially mortified that his mother's eyes had a curious flat glisten, as if she'd taken one of her antidepressant pills. He hoped she was aware of Ursula's presence. She said, in a tired voice, "Every eight minutes Pumpkin is on. I've timed it. Precisely. And the only caller so far was someone who hung up as soon as I answered."

Matt said grimly, "That's them. But they want me."

The four of them watched in silence as Pumpkin and the caption HAVE YOU SEEN ME? came on to the TV screen. Pumpkin was one of a melancholy sequence of "lost" pets. Her coat looked more sand coloured than golden, and her warm, intelligent brown eyes appeared demonic, reflecting a camera's red flash. Her tongue lolled from her mouth at a strange angle. She was sitting with her head raised, alert. Matt had taken the photo himself a few years ago. Weird, he thought, how photos are taken in all innocence and you could never guess how they might be one day used in newspapers, in obituaries.

Matt vowed he'd never again smile like an idiot for any camera.

Alex whispered, "I really let you down, Pumpkin. I wish..."

"It wasn't your fault, Alex," Matt said quickly.

"Yes, it was. It sure was."

Matt's mother began to speak, as if she hadn't been listening to this exchange. She was looking at Matt with her flat, glistening eyes. "I've tried to call your father. He's in San

Diego for the weekend, being interviewed. 'Wined and dined' as he says. But he is on a short list, I think. I mean, I think... this time, he *is*."

Matt and Alex exchanged glances: San Diego? Short list? Since when? "I wasn't sure if I should tell him anything more than that Pumpkin is missing. As if she'd wandered off..."

Matt said, "Right, Mom. That's a good idea."

"There's no point in upsetting him, after all. Is there."

It was a statement, not a question. No need to answer.

Matt drifted to the telephone as if he couldn't stay away from it. He lifted the receiver, intending to call the Rocky River police another time, but his mother said quickly, "Matt, no. You'll only antagonise them."

Matt protested, "But they're not doing anything. They're not looking for Pumpkin."

"How do you know that?"

"I *know*."

Matt's mother glanced nervously at Ursula, who stood with her arms folded self-consciously, leaning against an arm of the sofa near Alex. There was an air of unease between them, though Mrs Donaghy made an effort to smile at Ursula and Ursula smiled in return. Matt had never seen Ursula so subdued. If he hadn't known her better, he'd have thought she was – what? Shy? Ursula Riggs! And his mother, whose social manner was determinedly effervescent, as if she'd been trained as a girl to be bright and brisk and sunny, like a butterfly buffeted by the wind, seemed to be intimidated by Ursula, who was at least three inches taller than she, and more solidly built. Ursula wore only two gold studs in her ears this morning, but she was wearing her Mets cap, and her maroon satin Rocky River sports jacket, jeans and leather boots. With her short hair and blunt, snubnosed face, and those steely-blue eyes, you'd have to glance twice to see, yes, this is a *girl*. Matt had to smile. There was no one like Ursula. It intrigued him to see his mother observing Ursula, and to wonder what she thought. No one could have guessed that this tough-looking babe was the daughter of Clayton Riggs, CEO at Drummond, Inc. No one could have guessed that she lived in the most exclusive area of Rocky River.

"Ursula? Would you like some coffee, or – fruit juice? I'm sorry I've been so distracted," Matt's mother said.

"No thanks, Mrs Donaghy. But should I get you a little more coffee?"

Ursula was the one to bring the coffeepot to Matt's mother, and to carry it back to the kitchen. Matt's mother smiled again up at her, now with more animation. "Matt mentioned you're interested in – biology? And art?"

"I love art, yes. Wish I was better at it!"

"Do you draw? Paint?"

"Mainly draw."

"I majored in art history in college, at Barnard. American nineteenth century..."

"Do you know a painting by Edwin Elmer, *Mourning*? It's my favourite American painting, just about."

"Yes! I love that painting, too. It's so—"

"Haunting. Gives me shivers!"

To Matt's astonishment, there were Ursula and his

mother speaking animatedly about some nineteenth-century painting he'd never heard of. Matt couldn't believe that his mother was talking so knowledgeably: explaining how the artist Edward Elmer, who was self-trained, had composed the painting out of photographs. Mrs Donaghy had quit her part-time job for reasons of "health", and for the past several weeks she'd stayed home, tired, sallow skinned, and depressed, but now, talking with Ursula, she was smiling happily.

"Do you have pets, Ursula?"

"I wish I did, Mrs Donaghy, but – no. My dad likes to pretend he's allergic."

"You get very attached to them, you know."

"Oh, I know! I love Pumpkin, actually."

"Do you – know Pumpkin?"

"Well—"

Ursula glanced at Matt, who said awkwardly, "Mom, Ursula and I go hiking a lot. Pumpkin comes with us. Ursula's gotten to know her."

Ursula said, "She's a wonderful dog. She's – like a human being, actually." Ursula paused, and said vehemently, "No. She's a whole lot better than most human beings."

For a moment it looked as if Matt's mother was going to cry. Then she said, reaching for Ursula's hand, "It was so kind of you, dear, to testify on Matt's behalf. To the principal, and to the police. You made all the difference."

Ursula said quickly, "People didn't really believe that Matt was involved in anything crazy like that, Mrs Donaghy. Really, they didn't. It's just – like – some kind of mass hysteria. And then it got on TV."

"And now this – that has happened to Pumpkin. Because of those Brewer girls' lies."

"Because of the lawsuit, Mom," Matt said. "That's the reason."

Ursula glanced quickly at Matt, as if to appeal to him: don't be harsh with your mother! Not now.

In a sudden outburst of emotion Matt's mother said, "If only these terrible, cruel people would call us and tell us what they want... what they intend to do with Pumpkin. I can't bear this much longer!"

She began to cry. Shocking tears ran down her cheeks. Matt stood petrified, unable to respond, but Ursula went instinctively to Mrs Donaghy and put her arms around the smaller woman. Matt's mother was sobbing as if her heart were broken. "I always wished I had a daughter too, and not just sons. I miss a daughter. I'm so lonely here, sometimes, in this house...."

# forty-two

**I said to** Matt, "*I* have an idea. C'mon!"

"What?"

We were alone now, outside Matt's house in the driveway. I put my hands on his shoulders and looked him eye-to-eye. "Just tell me: who do you think took Pumpkin?"

There was a pause. Matt hesitated.

"I told you, Ursula. It could be almost anybody..."

"No! It's one person, with maybe some help. Who's that person?"

Again Matt paused. I could see in his eyes he knew.

I said, "My dad says in cases like this, if somebody is trying to harm you and you don't know who, just guess: the first person you name will probably be the guilty party. So – who?"

"...Trevor Cassity."

Trevor Cassity! This made sense.

But Matt had something to tell me that was unexpected.

"I never told you, Ursula, I've been kind of... ashamed. But Cassity and some of his friends cornered me a few weeks ago, and..." Matt was mumbling now, so I could hardly decipher his words, "sort of... beat up on me. I couldn't get away. It was hard for me to believe they hated me so, and wanted... really to hurt me. I kept thinking they'd stop. They called me 'fag' and taunted me about the lawsuit and... knocked me down. I wasn't really hurt," Matt said quickly, seeing the look in my face, "so I didn't tell anybody."

"You didn't tell anybody?"

"Like I said, I was sort of... ashamed."

"You didn't tell the police?"

"At the time, no. Last night I gave them Cassity's name, and a few others, to check out." Matt's mouth twisted bitterly. "I don't think the police took it very seriously. Pumpkin's only a *dog*."

I pulled at Matt, urging him to his car. "C'mon. We're going there."

"Going where?"

"Cassity's house. I know where he lives."

Matt balked. "Cassity's *house*? If he took Pumpkin, he wouldn't have her there. He's too smart for that."

"Matt, c'mon. We're going."

"But—"

"Do you want Pumpkin back safely, or what?"

"Of course, Ursula. But—"

Now I was pushing him. "C'mon."

*Ugly Girl, warrior-woman, in action!*

• • •

That morning when I was running out to go to Matt's house my mother called after me, "Ursula! Where on earth are you stampeding to?" and I shouted back, "Got to help out a friend, Mom." Mom called some question after me I couldn't hear, I was already out the door.

*Ugly Girl, helping out a friend.*

*Ugly Girl, hugging a friend's mom. Wild!*

I had to concede: Mrs Donaghy, when I first saw her, looked exactly like the kind of weepy wimpy female I can't stand, way, way worse than my own mom in her lousiest moods, but when I got to know her just a little, I liked her. I felt sorry for her. She was just sort of... soft. Like bread dough that hasn't been baked yet, to get a firm crust.

It wasn't like Ugly Girl to feel sorry for weakness, especially in somebody's mother (who should be strong, in my opinion), but Matt's mother was a nice person, I could tell. And smart.

And she was Matt's mother.

The Cassitys lived in a white colonial house with sort of fussy shutters and trim, a quarter mile from my house. In the circular driveway at the Cassitys' house there was a car that looked like a Lexus, and there was a larger vehicle that looked like a Land Rover. "See?" I said, excited. "That could be the SUV Alex saw." Matt was slow to switch off the ignition, like he was worried about what we were doing, but I was feeling the FIERY RED rising in my spine like liquid mercury. That rush you feel running out on to the basketball court or the hockey field. That rush that tells you *this is why I was born.*

Driving over, Matt was debating with me about the

wisdom of confronting Trevor Cassity like this. Sure, Cassity might have been involved in snatching Pumpkin – it was the sort of cruel, childish thing Cassity might do; but if so, he wouldn't have done it alone, and one of his friends probably had Pumpkin hidden away somewhere. She might be miles away in somebody's lodge in the mountains.... Strange: even an intelligent guy like Matt Donaghy must have some sort of macho pride, he's more afraid of making a fool of himself than of something really crucial, like his dog he loves getting hurt. Ugly Girl didn't give a damn for pride, at least not that kind.

"Hey, Matt. We want Pumpkin back safely, don't we?"

"Sure, but—"

I tried to be reasonable with Matt, I knew he'd been through a lot. He'd hardly slept last night. I said, "Would you rather sit around your house waiting for the phone to ring? Waiting for the police to come up with 'new developments'?"

"No, Ursula, but—"

"C'mon, then!"

I was out of Matt's car and halfway up the walk by the time Matt caught up with me. We were both breathing quickly, excited.

It was two twenty-four P.M. Pumpkin had been missing for about twenty hours. It seemed like a lot longer.

We rang the doorbell. After a while there came Trevor's father to open the door, looking surprised to see us. Especially to see me. "Ursula Riggs! Hel*lo*." Mr Cassity was wearing a sweatshirt and slacks and bifocal glasses I'd never seen on him before, which he quickly removed from his face. He smiled and blinked at me, puzzled.

Wondering what Clayton Riggs's daughter was doing, ringing his doorbell on a Saturday afternoon?

Matt introduced himself, but it didn't seem like Mr Cassity caught the name "Donaghy", or as if it meant anything to him. Mr Cassity was mostly looking at me.

Unlike my father, who kept in good condition considering his size and age, Mr Cassity was soft-looking in his face and body, like he was melting downward. He seemed confused by Matt's question, "Maybe you know why we're here, Mr Cassity?" and shook his head, no he did not, unless we wanted to see Trevor?

"Thanks, Mr Cassity," Matt said. "We sure would."

He invited us inside but we said we'd wait outside. We heard Mr Cassity calling "Trev-or!" up the stairs.

Weird: a jock like Trevor Cassity who carried himself so boastfully at school, who'd been bragging of his full-tuition sports scholarship to Tulane for next year, was just a kid who lived with his parents like the rest of us and he was upstairs in his room and his father summoned him downstairs calling, "Trev-or!" Like Trevor could be eight years old, not eighteen.

I nudged Matt, and Matt nudged me. We were both shaking. Maybe we were scared, but I preferred to think it was excitement, like before a big game.

"One of us should've staked out the back," I said, giggling. "Like on TV. If Trevor tries to escape."

Matt said, grinning, "I should've brought my Colt AR-15 assault rifle."

I pressed my hands over my ears. "I didn't hear that! I didn't hear a damned thing." We were losing control, everything was so funny.

But there came Trevor Cassity, led by his father, who was smiling and behaving like a genial Rocky River host. "Some friends of yours, Trev." Trevor was wearing a T-shirt with a soiled, stretched neck, and jeans and wool socks with no shoes, and wasn't looking very cool, like he'd just gotten up a few minutes ago. His eyes were bloodshot, staring at Matt and me. His mouth seemed to drop open, just perceptibly. Did he look guilty? We motioned for him to come outside, we wanted to talk to him, even as Mr Cassity invited Matt and me inside again – "Kids, it's too cold to stand out here on the stoop, c'mon in, please." I told Mr Cassity, politely as I could, that we didn't have time to visit, we just had to talk to Trevor for five minutes, and Mr Cassity was looking disappointed, like a kid nobody wants to play with. He said, "Well. Say hello to your father for me, Ursula, will you?"

So Trevor shut the door, not wanting his father to overhear, and tried to stare us down. "What do you want?" he asked. His voice quavered, I thought. Matt said, "You know what we want, Cassity," and I said, "Trevor, we've come for Matt's dog. We know you have her." Trevor tried to sneer, "Dog? What dog? You're crazy." Matt was clenching his fists, saying, "We know it was you and your buddies, so come on. We want Pumpkin back *now*." I'd never seen Matt so aggressive. I was fearful he'd lose control and jump at Trevor and they'd start fighting, and Trevor outweighed Matt by maybe twenty pounds, and Ugly Girl would have to get involved, and everything would be ruined.

I tried to keep my voice calm. "Trevor, everybody knows it was you. Your Land Rover was identified. There's a witness. We told the police we'd talk to you first. We don't want

anything to happen to Pumpkin, see? So tell us where she is."
Trevor was panting, as if he'd been running. He did look
frightened. But defiant and stubborn, too. Shaking his head
like we were totally crazy. Trying to laugh. "Look, I don't know
anything about any dog. Whose dog?"

I said, "Trevor, come on. This is serious."

Matt said, "If you've hurt Pumpkin, you'll be sorry. Where
is she?"

Trevor kept denying knowing anything about Pumpkin,
but he was getting more and more nervous. Had he really
thought he and his buddies could get away with this? Maybe
they'd been drunk and hadn't thought their plan through. I
told Trevor the police were getting a warrant to search houses
and property, and Trevor said, with his ugly laugh, "Go on! Let
'em try." So maybe Matt was right: they'd hidden Pumpkin
away somewhere. By the time she was found, she might have
starved to death.

Or she might be dead already.

I said, "If we don't get Pumpkin back by six tonight, I'm
going to tell on you."

"'Tell on me' – what?"

"Tell my dad."

Trevor's mouth quivered as if he wanted to laugh. But he
was catching on.

"You wouldn't want that, Trev, would you? My dad having
a serious conversation with your dad?"

"Look, Ursula, what's this got to do with *you*? This is
between Donaghy and me, and it's crazy anyway. Nobody can
prove a thing."

Trevor was looking worried now. Rubbing his hand over his stubbly chin. He was one of those guys who are considered good-looking – even sexy – but when you actually look at them close up, at a time like this, they don't exude much charm, only look like overgrown spoiled kids. I could see Trevor's eyes narrowing like a cornered rat's.

"Matt is my friend, and so is Pumpkin. Where is she?"

"I told you: I don't have Donaghy's dog. What'd I want with Donaghy's dog!"

Matt said, "You know where she is, though. Where?"

Trevor hesitated. He was trying to think. "Maybe I might... if I ask around."

Matt said, "Well, you'd better ask around, then. Right now."

Trevor protested, "I can't promise anything, because I don't *know*." He was sounding weak and unconvincing, though.

"We want Pumpkin back by six tonight, or I'm going to talk to my dad."

"That's sick! That's like something little kids would do."

"We *are* little kids."

"You can't prove this, Ursula! You know you can't."

"Why, because you and your buddies covered your tracks? Because you're smart? Well, we're smarter."

Trevor said, whining, "Why'd I want his dog?"

"Because you're cruel and stupid, that's why. Because you're a coward, terrorising an innocent animal."

"Yeah, well, *I* never threatened to blow up the school, or shoot a thousand people, and my folks aren't suing everybody for a hundred million dollars," Trevor said, his voice shaking.

He must've realised he'd said too much, for he stopped suddenly and mumbled, "Anyway you can't prove I had anything to do with it. There's plenty of guys, plenty of people, who hate Donaghy's guts, not just me."

I said, "I don't have to prove it. If I explain all this to my dad – how you've been harassing Matt at school, and you assaulted him, and now Pumpkin is missing – my dad will believe me. He will know that I'm right because I am right, and he won't require proof. And he'll punish you, for sure. He's a true dog lover! He'll punish you through your dad, whose job depends upon my dad's good opinion of him, be sure of it."

(Was this true? Just possibly. Ugly Girl was trembling so at this point, anything was possible.)

Trevor was looking more and more sick.

"In fact," I said, "I could talk to your father right now. I could explain the circumstances to him. He might like to intervene, before I talk to my father."

"No! Leave my father out of this."

Now Trevor was backing away. He'd stopped glaring at us and just wanted to escape.

I called after him, "Don't think it over too long, Trev. You have only till six tonight."

As Trevor shut the door, Matt said, "She better not be hurt, Cassity, or I'll—"

I grabbed Matt's arm and shook him. "Matt, no! Not a word more."

Amazingly, Matt shut his mouth.

*Big Mouth and Ugly Girl, warriors!*

# forty-three

**By four forty** p.m. that afternoon Pumpkin was back home. Safely.

The four of us – Matt, Alex, Mrs Donaghy and I – had been keeping a vigil in the Donaghys' family room, which overlooked the front and rear lawns of their property, and Alex was the first to sight the golden retriever slinking up the driveway. She'd been let out somewhere in the neighbourhood and had made her way home. "Pumpkin! There she is!" Alex yelled. We all ran outside to meet Pumpkin, even Mrs Donaghy, and what a relief it was to see that Pumpkin didn't appear hurt at all, only just nervous and confused. As soon as Matt and Alex knelt to hug her, though, she began barking joyously, licking their hands, her tail thrashing.

Inside, Pumpkin was fed her favourite dog foods, with much ceremony, and ate as if famished.

Where she'd been in those nightmare twenty-two hours, who had snatched her away, and what might have been done to her, Pumpkin would never disclose.

That night, just before I went to bed, I checked my e-mail and found this:

Sat 3/24/01  11:15 PM

Dear Ursula,
THANK YOU for saving my life!
I love you.

Your friend Pumpkin

# forty-four

*I love you.*

*And I love you.*

Ugly Girl wanted to hide her face, these words frightened her so much.

"Ursula! Come back. We miss you, and I bet you miss us."

This was so.

It didn't take much persuasion for Ms Schultz to talk me into rejoining the Rocky River High girls' basketball team.

I had to concede: Ugly Girl was restless without basketball, knowing that games were being played, and not as well played as they'd have been with me on the team. Not that I was Superwoman, but for girls' high school basketball I was pretty good. What I missed was my teammates, though I wouldn't have expected this; and the FIERY RED sensation that came over me just entering the locker room to change into my uniform, and all of us, the team, moving into the gym together. The feel of a basketball gripped in my hand.

If I made mistakes, if I missed baskets: OK. Ugly Girl would have to live with it, no different than the other girls.

It was strange about Ugly Girl. She was like a uniform, or a skin, I could slip into, but she wasn't right for all occasions. When I was with Matt, for instance. And once when I entered the gym, just after rejoining the team, some of the girls who were already there for practice turned to look at me, as if they'd been talking about me, and they laughed, and whistled and applauded and gave me the high five. "Urs-la! Riggs!" I half expected them to call me Ugly Girl.

It surprised me sometimes, that no one knew about Ugly Girl. She was my secret, even from Matt.

I rejoined in time for the last two games of the season, tough games with Peekskill and Ossining, last year's district champions. Rocky River's final game, with Ossining, was in the district tournament, and though we didn't win, we lost by only six points and it was a terrific, fast-paced game, well played on both sides, and something to be proud of.

I was high scorer for Rocky River, both games. But Courtney Levao played really well too. Courtney had a way of easing herself almost beneath the basket, and I'd pass to her, so swift we'd take everybody by surprise, and Courtney could leap up and sink the ball: smooth as a big cat! Courtney had stayed on as captain when I returned to the team, though she'd offered right away to resign. "Courtney, no!" I protested. I saw that the girls really liked her, and I thought, *That's a skill too: being liked. Getting along with people and respecting them. Ugly Girl could learn.*

For sure, Ugly Girl could learn. A lot.

I was slated to be captain next year, my senior year. I vowed I would not make the mistakes I'd made this year. I went to each of the girls on the team one by one and apologised for how I'd behaved. "I guess I basically forgot we're a team. Basketball isn't just one person." One of the girls laughed at me and said, teasing, "C'mon, Ursula. You don't mean that, you're just 'one person'?"

Bonnie LeMoyne laughed at me too. "I feel more comfortable with you being your obnoxious self, Urs, than this way. C'mon!"

*Urrsss.* That growly sound gave me the shivers – I loved it.

What was really wonderful about the games with Peekskill and Ossining, I had to admit, was that Matt Donaghy came to both of them, and sat in the front row of bleachers, and hardly took his eyes off me all the while I was on the court. At first I felt self-conscious, then, once the game began and the FIERY RED took over, I was OK. Each time I scored a basket, or passed the ball to another forward to score, Matt was on his feet clapping and cheering like he was the Rocky River team's biggest fan. In fact the team had larger crowds than usual, including guys from school for the first time in real numbers, which was flattering to us and great for morale. We'd even been written up in the local paper. Ms Schultz said we could be proud of ourselves and we were, and of her, too.

Mom and Lisa came to both games, to my surprise. Though I tried not to let on I was especially surprised. Lisa wasn't concentrating so much on her ballet lessons as she'd been; she'd said she was getting bored with ballet and wanted to do other things. Mom was disappointed, I could tell, but tried not to let Lisa sense it.

I teased Lisa: "If you grow twelve inches and gain like seventy pounds, maybe you'll be high scorer for girls' basketball in a few years. Just like Big Sis."

"Oh, Ursula!" Lisa said, taking this seriously. "I could never play any sport like *you*."

Maybe that was so. Lisa wasn't an Ugly Girl. It didn't mean so much to her to win, win, win.

After the Ossining game I introduced Matt to my mother and Lisa. It was a little awkward. I saw Mom blink at Matt, who was obviously not the troublemaker she'd been expecting: with his boyish, freckled face, his slightly shy manner, and his politeness. "Hi Mrs Riggs! Ursula says some really cool things about you."

Mom's jaw practically dropped. "Ursula does?"

Lisa giggled at this, and suddenly we were all laughing, even Matt. I don't know what was so funny.

Mom took me aside and said, "That boy is so sweet! He's nothing like... well, you know."

I told Mom that Matt and I were going out to get something to eat, and Matt would be driving me home, and Mom said impulsively, squeezing my hand like a little girl, "Come with us. Please! It's my treat."

• • •

Just about the coolest thing about that day was my dad had called earlier, before the game, from Tokyo. He wanted to tell me he was thinking of me, and he "really, really wished" he could have made the game. I wiped at my eyes. This was so corny and weird! "Dad, come *on*. There's nowhere you'd want to be less than a high school basketball game, and you know it."

"Honey, you are W-R-O-N-G. I can immediately think of" – he pretended to be counting on his fingers so that I could hear – "four, five – six – places I'd definitely want to be less."

"Oh, Dad! That's mean."

I don't know why I was crying, I was so happy.

# forty-five

**fire alarms were** ringing, deafening.

"Fire drill!"

On the Thursday following the girls' basketball game with Ossining, there was a sudden rude interruption of fourth period at Rocky River High.

Only a routine fire drill – or was it?

The 2307 Rocky River students knew from past experience (or thought they knew) that this was only a boring fire drill and not a real fire (they didn't smell smoke – did they?), but still there was an atmosphere of excitement and apprehension. It might be on the TV news that night: Rocky River High going up in flames! For some of the less mature boys it was an occasion for mirth. (What's so funny about a fire drill? *It just is.*) For others the relentless ring-ring-ringing of the alarms made their heartbeats quicken unpleasantly. Like Ecstasy – but no music. There were girls who pressed the palms of their hands against their ears, complaining of migraine headaches coming on. In each classroom and in the gym, library, study halls everyone was on their feet, gathering up books and backpacks. Teachers assumed looks of calm sobriety.

"Students, line up quietly. File out in order. No pushing. Careful on the stairs. Let's go."

There came Mr Parrish's voice over the loudspeaker. This was routine-fire-drill stuff. Mr Parrish speaking in his earnest, forced-calm, paternal voice meant to reassure. Though some of the guys had to laugh, and mimicked him: "Move along quickly, students. This is an emergency situation but there is no cause for panic. Follow your teachers' instructions precisely. Do not go to your lockers. I repeat: do not go to your lockers...."

*Do not go to your lockers!* The mimicry sounded like demented parrots throughout the school.

In Mr Bernhardt's German I class in room 229 Matt Donaghy was more shaken than the other students by the sudden eruption of noise. He swallowed hard, hoping this wouldn't be blamed, somehow, on him.

Obediently, Matt grabbed up his backpack and marched with the others, row by row, for the most part silently, out of the classroom with its big map of Germany at the front of the room, and into the corridor where the alarms were really loud. Mr Bernhardt directed them, exulting in his Teutonic authority, shouting – "Move right along, students! *Macht schnell!*" Trying to contain their excitement, they marched down the stairs and outside into dismal weather, icy rain, sleet. And wind. "What a bummer!" a boy complained to Matt. "They should let us get our coats at least." A number of classrooms had already emptied out, and more were on their way. Matt was always amazed how quickly hundreds of human beings could be mobilised to *move*. Still, the fire alarms were ringing.

Except: something was wrong. This wasn't routine. Emergency vehicles were pulling up the circular drive in front of the school, Rocky River police cars, a fire truck, ambulances. Ambulances! Had someone been hurt? What was this? Instead of marching out on to the school grounds, standing in rows as teachers took attendance, and waiting dutifully to be led back into the school, 2307 students were being hurriedly marched off the school grounds entirely, into the cordoned-off street and beyond.

A TV crew was setting up cameras in the street. Overhead – was that a police helicopter?

Walking quickly, worried now, Matt looked around for Ursula. Fourth period – Ursula's art class. He couldn't find her. What was happening? On all sides kids were panicking and beginning to run. There were shouts: "Bomb!" – "Bomb threat!" – "Bomb's gonna go off!"

A bomb!

Now Matt Donaghy would surely be blamed.

In fact, no bomb went off that afternoon.

The emergency would turn out to be, as media headlines would designate it, a bomb scare, not an actual bomb.

At the time, though, the scene was mass confusion. Students were urged to go immediately home, classes were cancelled for the rest of the day. Police and firemen were setting up blockades around the building at a presumably safe distance. A Westchester County bomb squad arrived and prepared to enter the building. Already, anxious parents were arriving to take their children home. Yet some were reluctant to go home, preferring to mill about in the icy rain, coatless, hatless, shivering, talking excitedly with one another. A bomb? Where? What kind? As a Rocky River cheerleader said, interviewed by a local TV station for the six-o'clock news, "It was the first bomb threat in the history of Rocky River High and it does make you feel kind of... *important*."

"Matthew Donaghy!" – there came Mr Parrish in Matt's direction, in a plastic raincoat, glasses streaming moisture. He looked like an old, ravaged man. Matt saw that he was accompanied by a plainclothes Rocky River detective. Matt had an impulse to turn and run.

Mr Parrish was explaining that Rocky River police were going to take Matt into protective custody and drive him home. Matt protested, "Mr Parrish, this wasn't me! I don't have anything to do with this! Please." He was close to crying. He was close to striking at these men with his fists. The detective laid a hand on Matt's shoulder, to calm him, or to restrain him, and said, "Son, we know it wasn't you. You were in class when the call came in. Don't be upset, OK? We're going to take you home."

Matt stammered, "I am upset. I – what is this?"

"We're taking you into protective custody and we're driving you home. This way."

Matt objected, "But I didn't do anything. You just said."

"But you might be in danger, Matthew. Whoever the anonymous caller is, the call is related to you."

"To me? How?"

"This way, son. Through here."

And so, for the second time in just over two months, Matt Donaghy was observed being led to a Rocky River squad car and urged inside. (Arrested? Again? Was he cuffed? Was he forced into the squad car?) Miserably, Matt had no choice but to obey. As he climbed into the rear of the car, he saw a ring of students watching him, staring avidly. Some were familiar faces from his German class. And there was Skeet Curlew, gaping. Skeet! Matt grinned. He had a wild impulse to raise his fist to Skeet in the notorious Black Power salute, and maybe Skeet would be taken away too. Maybe a photographer could catch the moment.

But no: Big Mouth resisted.

Thurs 3/29/01  5:20 PM

Dear Ursula,

It's your friend Matt in "protective custody"--"for my own safety"-- but at home, at least. I AM NOT ARRESTED.

I looked for you in that wild scene & couldn't see you.
I hope you were OK during our "evacuation".

Everybody expecting a bomb to go off at any minute. But the latest news is, I guess, there was no bomb. At least, nobody can find a bomb.

Pumpkin's here & says HELLO to you. Pumpkin is really REALLY glad she isn't a member of the species Homo sapiens who are collectively & individually CRAZY.

I don't know what people are saying about Matt Donaghy, but the reason I was taken into protective custody is: the guy who called the school about the bomb said, "This time I'm going to do the job right." Police believe this is in reference to me. That the caller was pretending to be me. (Except he called at a really dumb time, when I was in Bernhardt's German class.)

The office at school tapes all their incoming calls now. Since January. Evidently they got a lot of weird calls then.

Anyway, I'm in protective custody but probably not for long. With the tape, & a smart way they have of tracking phone calls, they expect to catch the bomber/ caller very soon.

(Not T. Cassity & his buddies, I bet. You'd have to be totally crazy to pull a stunt like this.)

I'm worried about Mom, mostly. She was sort of freaked out when they brought me home. Luckily, they called her first from the squad car. She started screaming at them, "Why are you persecuting us?" & the detective & I had to both try to calm her. We were saying it was a "routine procedure"--"protective custody"--but Mom just cried.

Dad is flying home right away this time. I'm hoping that will be a GOOD THING.

Love,

Matt

Fri 3/30/01  6:47 AM

Dear Ursula,

The anonymous caller is: Reverend Brewer.

Police just informed us. He's been arrested. Call me as soon as you read this, OK?

Love,
Matt

# forty-six

**EVEN as it** was being released to the media, the news was spreading through Rocky River High.

Two items of news, in fact.

First, the bomb scare. An anonymous caller had telephoned the school at the start of the fourth period of the previous day with a warning that a bomb was on the premises timed to detonate "within the hour". The caller added cryptically, "This time I'm going to do the job right." No bomb was located, however, and the call was quickly traced to Reverend Brewer, who'd used a pay phone a few blocks from his church, hoping to disguise his voice by speaking through wadded cloth. Brewer's voice, taped, was identified by forensic scientists; the call was traced to the pay phone, where Brewer's fingerprints were found, and to Brewer's astonishment he was arrested and charged with a felony, and his bail set at $500,000.

The second item of news: Matthew Donaghy's parents announced through their attorney that they were dropping their controversial lawsuit in its entirety. The reason being: "Mr and Mrs Donaghy no longer believe that litigation is the best way to pursue justice."

Fri 3/30/01  6:37 PM

30 mars
dear matt,
such good news/ i'm happy for you

call me when you can

love,
u r

april

# forty-SEVEN

"oh, ursula."

This was Mom's reaction. She just stared. I saw her swallow hard and a swarm of thoughts rush through her head she decided not to articulate. Lisa loved my new look – "Ursula, wow! Cool" – and kept stealing glances at me through dinner, and reaching over to touch my hair. But Dad was the one who really, like, reacted. He was on a new, modified schedule that allowed him to have dinner with his family at least two nights a week, so it was like a holiday time anyway, and we were feeling good about that, so Dad comes home and sees me and stares and blinks and tries to be funny, to hide his surprise, adjusting his glasses to peer at me, and finally he hugs me and says, "Kiddo, you're a rare one. I have to admit you look glamorous. But intimidating, too. Like an Amazon rock star."

I was flattered by this, but protested, "Dad, I don't want to look like some rock star, I just want to look like *me*."

Dad laughed. "Ursula, you do."

What I'd done was: a few days after Reverend Brewer's arrest, I made a secret appointment with a hair salon in Rocky River and had my hair cut really short in back and longer on the sides, in sleek, sweeping wings, and bleached platinum blonde.

This was to celebrate, I was feeling so good. I was tired of my old dirty-blonde hair that didn't reflect this good feeling.

*Ugly Girl's new look.*

*Ugly Girl will always surprise.*

When Matt saw me, he was nearly as shocked as Dad. Almost, his jaw dropped.

"Ursula, you look... terrific. Maybe I should bleach my hair too."

"Why don't you?"

Matt laughed. How would Matt Donaghy look with platinum blonde hair instead of his familiar faded-red hair? "Maybe if my play is chosen for the festival. We could both perform in it then."

This was a new idea, and I liked it. I'd never been on a stage in my life except in grade school, but I believed it wouldn't be too different from sports, with people staring at you. With Ugly Girl cool and new blonde hair, and reciting Matt's comic dialogue, I knew I would love it.

Matt had revised his play *William Wilson: A Case of Mistaken Identity* and submitted it for the Spring Arts Festival next month. I hadn't seen the earlier version, which he said was "juvenile", but this one was extremely clever and funny. There were just two characters, both named "William Wilson" (like in the story by Edgar Allan Poe); one is evil and the other is good – the "voice of conscience". Matt read the role of W 1 and I read the role of W 2 – we tried to approximate the same deep throaty baritone voice – and it was hard to keep from breaking down laughing, the dialogue was so funny. The essence of Matt's play is that William Wilson 1 has a big mouth that gets him into trouble and William Wilson 2 is always trying to remedy things, explain things, save W 1 from disaster. But while W 1 is a big mouth, he's also pretty shrewd, too. An amplifier picks up his words and magnifies and distorts them so it's like he has said the opposite of what he meant to say. Finally it's too much for W 2, who turns into a Big Mouth himself and the two of them speak in unison as sirens and whirling red lights close in upon them...

I was proud of Matt. Maybe I was even a little surprised that he could write that well.

Another comic piece Matt wrote for the *Rocky River Run* was more serious: 'Mass Media Hysteria.' This was so excellent, I urged him to send it to *The New York Times*'s op-ed page. Matt was shocked at my suggestion. "They'd never publish anything I wrote.... I'm just a high school kid in Westchester."

I said, "Oh, Matt. The worst they can do is reject it." I told him I'd fax the piece to the paper myself if he didn't want to, and Matt said he'd think it over.

Around school everybody stared at us kind of openly now. Not just my new look, but Matt and me together. Mostly, people were friendly. Like we'd all come through a bad time and it was a new season now, right?

# forty-eight

**Was Matt imagining** it? Or was it real?

Overnight – well, almost overnight – things were changing for him at Rocky River High.

For weeks he'd been moving like a ghost among his classmates, drawing surreptitious glances and stares but not many smiles, and now people were beginning to acknowledge him again. As if he'd returned from the Land of the Dead.

He told Ursula, "Must be I'm off the blacklist now. Guess I should be grateful, huh?"

Ursula laughed. She felt exactly as Matt did about the situation.

"Well, dropping the lawsuit was a good idea, you know."

Matt had to agree. Dropping the lawsuit had changed everything.

And the revelations in the media about Reverend Brewer, who'd not only telephoned in a fake bomb threat to the school but conspired to blame it on Matt Donaghy.

Muriel and Miriam Brewer had been involved too. Exactly how police weren't revealing because the girls were minors but suddenly the Brewer twins were gone from school. Their desks and lockers emptied out.

Ursula said, "Almost, I feel sorry for them, not graduating. With a father like that teaching them hate."

Matt was quiet. Sure he'd like to forgive the Brewers, he'd like to forgive all meanness and evil, but it wasn't that easy if you've been hurt. And though Matt was in a good mood these days, he'd remember the hurt for a long time. "I guess," he said, dubiously.

She was getting to know Matt so well, sometimes they had only to glance at each other to share a thought. Especially a satirical thought when someone was being conspicuously "nice" to Matt.

The editors of the literary magazine and their advisor, Mel Steiner, invited Matt to resume his humour column – "Your fans miss you, Matt."

Matt pondered what to write for them. He was embarrassed to discover, when he reread a copy of "Just for the Record", the satirical piece he'd written in a black bitter mood in February, that it wasn't very good after all. It was raw, childish, clumsy. A joke about lethal injection that came off like self-pity. Mr Steiner had been right to reject it.

Still, Matt wasn't sure if he could be "funny" again, in his old easygoing way.

*Big Mouth, popular? But why?*

Since Ursula was intimidating, especially now with her glaring-blonde hair, and her manner that differed so from most girls' soft-melting, sunny-cheery smiles, people tended to approach Matt more readily when he was alone.

Russ Mercer was speaking to him again, and often. Cal Carter asked Matt about track practice, as if it were just the other day they'd been friends. ("No. I'm not on the team this season," Matt said. "I'm concentrating on my writing.") There was Neil Donaghue asking for helpful hints regarding the maths assignment, and there was Skeet Curlew, looking a little embarrassed, suggesting lamely that they get together sometime soon. ("Sure," Matt said. "Not this weekend, though. I'm kind of busy.") There was Sandy Friedman in her usual rush pausing to squeeze Matt's arm and assure him that she really, really missed him at student council meetings – "You were, like, the voice of reason."

And there was Stacey Flynn twisting a strand of hair around her forefinger. Hesitant to approach Matt, but knowing she should. Matt had to concede that Stacey was a very pretty girl. He didn't want to think she was shallow, that she'd hurt him; he was thinking instead that she'd gotten prettier since – well, since Matt's trouble. Since they'd last spoken. Stacey was wearing a yellow cotton knit sweater, and her dark glossy hair fell in sweeping curtains around her heart-shaped face. She was a slender, petite girl who craned her neck becomingly to gaze up at boys, as she was gazing up at Matt, standing at his locker and asking him what had become of the play he'd adapted from the Edgar Allan Poe story – "Did you submit it to the festival?"

Originally, Stacey had been going to perform in Matt's play.

Matt said, "It's revised now. It's very different."

"But it was wonderful before..."

"Was it?" Matt asked, frowning. Stacey's proximity made him nervous. He felt that people were watching them. Yet he could hardly shut his locker and move away, Stacey was standing so close.

"It was! You have a real gift for comedy."

"Better that than a gift for tragedy, I guess."

Stacey didn't know how to interpret this enigmatic remark. Matt, turning away, wasn't sure what it meant either.

Wed 4/11/01  8:10 PM

Dear Matt,

It's hard for me to say this. I guess it's an apology.

I can't explain why I didn't speak to you for so long.

I felt so badly about it, all the while.

I could blame my folks, I guess. (They didn't want me to "get involved". They're worried about my college applications and letters of recommendation already, can you believe it???)

But really it's my fault.

Call me sometime if you want to talk. Whenever.

Your friend,
Stacey

There were other e-mails from his old friends. And unexpected invitations.

One weekend, Matt was invited to a party at Cal Carter's house. He hesitated before saying, maybe, maybe he'd come – "If I can bring Ursula Riggs."

Cal was an old friend from middle school. Something of a jock, on the swimming team. A solid B-plus student, always popular with girls. Cal said, tactlessly, "Ursula *Riggs*? You want to bring *her*?"

"Yes," Matt said, annoyed, "I want to bring Ursula."

Cal said uncomfortably, "Ursula's cool, but... she wouldn't fit in too well, would she? I mean... with us?"

Matt said, "Then I wouldn't fit in with 'us' either."

Slamming his locker and walking away to leave Cal staring after him.

*Phonies. Hypocrites. Ursula's worth all of you put together.*

The most unexpected invitation was to Brooke Tyler's seventeenth birthday party, to be held at the Rocky River Yacht Club. Brooke was in Matt's history class, and dated a popular senior; her father was a well-known CBS TV producer. Matt didn't know Brooke well but was flattered by the invitation.

More than flattered, Matt was elated.

It was the first time Brooke Tyler or her clique had ever invited Matt Donaghy anywhere.

But when Matt asked if he could bring Ursula, he saw Brooke frown just perceptibly and say, with her guileless cheerleader smile, "Ursula *Riggs*? She's, like, your girl?"

"Ursula is my friend."

Brooke relented, saying, "Sure, bring Ursula. That's cool."

But Ursula didn't think it was so cool when Matt asked her.

"Those phonies! Are you serious?"

Matt shook his head, embarrassed.

"Let's go to New York instead," Ursula said. There was a new play that had just opened in the Village, which she thought they'd both like. "'Wild, irreverent, funny but profound' – the review made it sound like something Matt Donaghy might've written."

# forty-nine

"Pump-kin! This way."

She was trotting into the woods, panting and sniffing happily. It was late April, a chilly spring, but mostly everything had thawed and there was that fresh moist smell of earth and last year's leaves and Rocky River Creek was rushing downhill in a cascade of whitewater ripples. The sky was so blue! As usual Matt and I hiked without talking much. Mainly we'd point out things to each other to see, like the view of the Hudson River, or a spectacular formation of shale outcropping like something carved. The nature preserve was like a prehistoric place – I think that's why we loved it. And felt safe there.

The hard part of humanity is history. All that's been done to human beings by other human beings. In the Rocky River Nature Preserve you didn't have to think of such things.

I wondered if Matt wanted to hike to the ravine where I'd

discovered him that day. I wondered if that was what he'd intended, bringing us here for his "surprise revelation".

I hoped not. I was thinking it would be better to forget that. "'Forget and forgive' – " Matt liked to joke. "Or 'forgive and forget'. Whatever."

Matt was being mysterious, telling me he had something to reveal and wanted to tell me in our special place.

We'd packed a big lunch. Hiking made both of us really hungry.

By accident (or anyway I think it was an accident) I realised this day in April was approaching an anniversary for us: almost three months since the evening u r sent Matt Donaghy the message *please call me, its urgent.*

Pumpkin was overjoyed to come with us. Since the kidnapping she'd become more puppylike, dependent upon Matt, and me. She was afraid to be alone and shied away from strangers, sudden noises and movements, like cars on the street, or airplanes high overhead. Matt said she trembled and whimpered in her sleep like she was trying to run but couldn't – "Like a human nightmare, you know the kind?" We hugged Pumpkin a lot to assure her she was safe, and she was loved.

Sometimes I'd see this look in Matt's face, and I knew he was thinking of Trevor Cassity and those guys, what they'd done to him and to Pumpkin; how they'd terrorised her, and she'd never be the same dog again; and how out of pure meanness they'd made the Donaghys' lives miserable for those hours. I respected Matt too much to try to cajole him out of it, these emotions belonged to him legitimately, but I would try to change the subject as soon as I could. Ugly Girl was learning there's no point in dwelling on the past and brooding, replaying old hurts and humiliations in your head.

I was relieved – we didn't hike to the very top of the ravine.

We'd been walking for about an hour when we decided to stop for lunch, and called Pumpkin back. But suddenly we were hearing voices – kind of loud, jarring voices – somewhere close by. We glanced at each other. A single sensation passed through us. *No. Not here.* Matt's jaw tightened, and I felt my heart beat hard, and I made sure that Pumpkin was safely back with us, licking and nudging against my hand. Some quick terrible fantasy of Pumpkin attacked by another dog, or kids from Rocky River showing up to spoil our outing, ran through my head... but only for a moment. The voices were fading, the hikers had taken another trail. The sound of Rocky River Creek drowned out the disturbance.

We sat on a broad, sloping granite boulder that looked as if it had emerged out of the sea a million years ago. It had a curious striated texture like seaweed, and a briny smell. I had an impulse to lay my cheek against it. It was warm, comfortingly warm, from the sun. Though the air was chilly, the boulder's surface was heated. Sunshine fell on our uplifted faces. I'd made tuna fish sandwiches with pitta bread and numerous raw vegetables and bean sprouts and Matt teased me about being a vegetarian – "Is a tuna fish a giant vegetable?" I laughed and refused to answer.

Matt reminded me of my dad, I realised. Though they hadn't yet met. He respected me but didn't take me overly seriously. If Ugly Girl had pretensions, both Matt Donaghy and Clayton Riggs knew how to tease her, gently.

It was then that Matt told me his good news: "Ursula, *The New York Times* is going to publish my column on the op-ed page. Thanks to you."

"Oh, Matt. What wonderful news."

I stared at him. I was happy, and yet – I felt a little envious, too.

"And what's even more exciting: *William Wilson* will be in the Spring Festival. Which means that Ursula Riggs will make her theatrical debut in about five weeks."

"Matt! Congratulations."

"No. You were my inspiration."

Suddenly we were hugging. Pumpkin, who was dozing off on the rock, woke up, somehow got between us, and began to thrash her tail excitedly. I felt like crying, but that was ridiculous. Matt hugged me so hard, the breath rushed out of me. Rocky River Creek roared in my ears. Matt ducked his head and pressed his mouth against mine and we were both breathing quickly, and not quite prepared.

The first kiss didn't work out too well, I guess. We'd be trying others.

Ted van Lieshout

# brothers

Can you still be a brother when your brother is dead? Luke often wonders. His brother Marius has died, leaving Luke alone with their parents. When their mother decides to burn Marius's belongings in a ceremonial bonfire, Luke saves his brother's diary and makes it his own by writing in it. And so begins a dialogue between the brothers, the dead and the living, from which truths emerge, truths of life and death and love.

Acclaim from the International Press:
"Van Lieshout has written, in clear and simple language, one of the most beautiful books for adolescents I have read in ages."

*An imprint of* HarperCollins*Publishers*

PATRICIA *cut* McCORMICK

*Most of the girls are anorexic. They're called guests with food issues. Some are druggies. They're called guests with substance abuse issues. The rest, like me, are assorted psychos. We're called guests with behavioural issues. And the place is a residential treatment facility. It is not called a loony bin.*

Callie isn't speaking to anybody. Instead she watches and listens, absorbing and analysing everything that goes on at 'Sick Minds', the place where she was sent because she cuts herself. Yet Callie finds herself drawn into the lives of the other guests. And discovers she has power over life and death...

"I read *Cut* in one breathless sitting... You will not soon forget a girl named Callie and this remarkable novel."
*Robert Cormier*

((Collins flamingo

An *imprint* of HarperCollins*Publishers*

# DISCONNECTED

## SHERRY**ASHWORTH**

*"It's hard to know where to begin. I'm not even sure who I want to talk to. Or what I want to say. But maybe if I try to put all the different parts together it will make some sort of sense. So here's my story, and it's for each of you to whom I owe an explanation. But remember, I'm not sorry."*

Catherine Margaret Holmes
Loving and dutiful daughter.

Cathy Holmes
A-level, A-grade student.

Cath Holmes
Friend and confidante.

Cat
Risk taker, thrill seeker, rebel.

*Will that do as an introduction?*

"It's not often that a book makes me think I must go out and find some more of this author's work now, but that's the effect *Disconnected* had on me. I was well and truly blown away."
*Fiona McKinlay, teenage reviewer for whsonline.co.uk*

*An imprint of HarperCollinsPublishers*

# zero%

## Mark Swallow

*I hereby dedicate my Business Studies GCSE to my father. I don't need it because, Dad, I am the business.*

Jack is fed up with other people's decisions. Can't he run his life on his own terms? He's pretty famous at school – Jack Curling, entrepreneur and wheeler-dealer. Still his dad can't see that he's OK doing it his way. So it's time to prove a point. The exam is waiting. Can Jack score precisely zero per cent?

"A sassy book with some strong language and a lot of verve."
*The Observer*

**Collins flamingo**

⬛ *An imprint of HarperCollinsPublishers*

# Breakers

## Julia Clarke

*Bianca is dressed in white, like a delicate oriental bird that has landed here by accident. Before she speaks she lights a cigarette. She only smokes when she's upset. 'We're going to have a complete break from London. We're leaving.'*

Cat no longer recognises her life. Uprooted from the city by their actress mother, she and her younger sister Ana must adapt to living by the sea in Yorkshire. Nothing is the same – it's hard to tell friends from enemies, and truth from lies. Soon Cat finds herself caught up in conflicts as powerful as the breakers pounding the shore…

"Unsentimental, gritty and funny, there's only one possible result: Teenagers 1, Parents 0."
*achuka.co.uk*

Collins flamingo
*An imprint of HarperCollinsPublishers*

# ALCHEMY

## *MARGARET MAHY*

*"I am Quando the Magician!" the man cries. "I work enchantments. But never forget – it is your job to work out just where the trick leaves off and the true magic begins."*

Roland has everything a young man could wish for – good looks, enough money, a ready wit, sexy girlfriend and a perfect school record. So the fact that he committed a petty crime is something he can hardly explain to himself, let alone anyone else. Worse still, Mr Hudson, his teacher, knows all about it, and uses this knowledge to blackmail Roland into befriending misfit Jess Ferret. But when Jess doesn't repond to Roland's confident advances, he becomes intrigued with the girl for his own reasons...

Self-empowerment meets the super-natural in this astonishing new novel from this internationally acclaimed, multiple award-winning novelist.

((Collins flamingo

An *imprint of* HarperCollins*Publishers*

# THE KILLER'S COUSIN

## NANCY WERLIN

*"Tell me," Lily said, as if casually. "How did it feel when she went down?"* All the air left the room. Lily was leaning forward, her gaze avid, sucking at mine. *"Did you feel... powerful? Even for a minute?"*

Recently acquitted of murder, David has moved to Massachusetts to stay with his aunt and uncle and complete his senior year of high school. But his aunt makes it clear that he is not welcome in their house, and his young cousin Lily is viciously hostile. As Lily's behaviour becomes increasingly threatening, David wonders what secrets lurk within her. And the more he thinks about Lily, the more he is forced to deal with the horrors of the past.

Winner of the Edgar Allan Poe Award, *The Killer's Cousin* chills and thrills on every page.

((Collins flamingo

*An imprint of HarperCollinsPublishers*

# IN THE MIDDLE OF THE NIGHT

## Robert Cormier

*Do not pick up the phone. Let your mother or me answer it. If it's for you, I will hand it over. Alone in the house, you do not answer.*

The phone calls come every year, waking Denny up in the middle of the night. Every year, Denny's father calmly answers. He never speaks. He simply listens. But this year it's different. It's twenty-five years since the fire, the terrible tragedy for which Denny's father bears the blame. The tragedy which triggered these calls, year in, year out. This year, Denny has had enough. This year, he will pick up the phone – and face the consequences.

Shortlisted for the Carnegie Medal.

"One of the most tautly written and frightening of Robert Cormier's always scary novels."
*Independent*

((Collins flamingo

*An imprint of HarperCollinsPublishers*